Kaillar

Morris Fenris

Kaillar, Three Brothers Lodge #3

Table of Contents

Prologue

Four and half years earlier, Pe'ahi, Maui, Hawaii...

Becca Edwards sat silently as her soon-to-be ex-boyfriend parked his Jeep at the top of the beach. Without even looking at her, he slammed the vehicle off and jumped from the driver's side. He grabbed his surfboard from the back, then stopped at the door to the vehicle, and she could feel him staring at her.

It took everything she had left in her to keep her eyes forward and not look at him. *If I look at him, I'm going to throw up. Don't look at him. Just ignore him and he'll leave, and then you can deal with it.*

"Becca, do yourself a favor and wash your face before you come down to the beach. You look awful." He waited for her acknowledgement, and when it didn't come, he slammed his fist on the side of the vehicle, the unexpected noise making her jump and emit a soft cry of fear.

"Whatever!" He grabbed his board, and headed towards the beach, and the blue water beyond.

Becca stared straight ahead, willing the tears brimming in her eyes not to fall. He'd already made her cry once; she wasn't going to let him have the satisfaction of seeing her cry a second time today.

Dagan Carlson was an up-and-coming surfer, coming in second place in the World Championships the year before. This year, he was pushing himself to take on bigger and stronger waves, determined to come out on top at the end of the season.

Becca had met him at the end of the previous season, but since she wasn't even out of high school yet, they'd done nothing more than flirt a bit. He was a star, and had gorgeous, bikini clad girls throwing themselves at him all the time. Something that had bothered Becca immensely.

They'd started emailing each other over the summer months, and then he'd announced that he was coming back to Hawai'i to train during the winter. She'd done everything in her power to persuade him to stay on the Big Island, and it seemed to have worked. He'd booked several bungalows at her parents' resort for himself and his surfing buddies. Becca had been ecstatic when she'd heard the news.

She'd done what she could to keep track of him once he arrived. Her brother, Kevin, and his best friend Kalino had helped in that regard. At the age of fourteen each, they were the reigning Island Junior Champions, and showed great promise for taking on the bigger waves once they became more mature. Getting to surf alongside someone of Dagan's caliber was every teenage surfer's dream.

Hawaii was full of great surf spots, and since Kalino's dad happened to own and operate a charter flight service, getting around the islands was cheap and easy. Today the boys were surfing at Pe'ahi. The islanders and surfers alike reverently referred to the waves that crashed upon her shores as "Jaws" because if you weren't prepared, she would chew you up, and you'd be lucky if she spit you back out.

The waves at Pe'ahi were some of the strongest and biggest in the world, and both Kevin and Kalino had been warned by their parents to stay inside on the smaller waves. The boys weren't stupid, and there was no doubt in anyone's mind that they would take great care in these more dangerous waters.

Becca had tagged along for the day after making plans to meet up with Dagan for an early lunch. He'd been island hopping for the last month, training, but also playing quite a bit. He'd taken an interest in Becca, and she'd returned it wholeheartedly, much to her parents' dismay.

Her mother had been adamantly against her spending any time with the cocky surfer who was four years older than her daughter was. But Becca had a big case of puppy love, and hadn't taken any of her mother's warnings to heart. Warnings that had come to fruition just a short while before, forever changing her life in a not so pleasant way. Innocence almost lost, and trust and a belief in happily ever after seemed very far away right now.

Realizing that she'd been sitting in the Jeep too long, she carefully wiped the tears from her cheeks, wincing when she touched the spot on her cheek that would probably show a bruise in the morning. She swallowed carefully, her throat sore from where Dagan's hands had wrapped themselves around it while he…

She took a deep breath, and then slipped from the vehicle. *I should be grateful that park ranger came along when he did, or I'd have more than a sore cheek, split lip, and sore throat.*

Dagan had been pushing her to move forward with their physical relationship for the last week, but Becca had held fast to her convictions. Convictions that Dagan hadn't even tried to honor not even an hour ago. He'd become another person, shoving her down into the soft sand, and choking her as he tried to pull her clothing off her body. *Come on Becca. I promise you'll like it if you just try it. Don't be such a prude!*

Her thin cotton shirt and cut off jean shorts over her bikini were little barrier to his searching hands. She'd struggled, and he'd slapped her across the face to keep her quiet. She'd yelled anyway, bringing her knee up in an effort to get him off her, and that's when the park ranger had called out.

Dagan had quickly risen to his feet, chuckling when the park ranger had looked at them as naughty children. Becca had been so embarrassed; she'd kept her face hidden until the ranger had left. She'd rushed back to Dagan's rental Jeep, and demanded that he take her back to the beach.

Dagan had assured her they would have plenty of time to finish things later that evening. The surfers were planning to camp out on the beach so they could catch the early morning waves. Becca and the two boys had gained permission to do so as well, with a promise that Kalino's dad would be heading back to the Big Island around suppertime should they change their minds.

Becca didn't mention to Dagan that she was grabbing her brother and Kalino and heading straight for the airport. Even if they had to wait on Kalino's father to pick them up for hours, she wanted nothing to do with Dagan Carlson. Ever again. Whatever infatuation she'd had for him was gone, right along with her ability to trust.

As she walked down to the beach, searching for her brother, she found him, but she hadn't realized how badly bruised her face had already become. Kevin knew she'd taken off with Dagan, and he instantly jumped to the right conclusion.

"I'll kill him!" He'd turned, searching the beach, and then he'd taken off running for the water. For being her younger brother, he was fiercely protective of his sister, and with that went a lack of self-control that oftentimes scared Becca.

"Kevin! Don't! Let's just leave!" Becca chased him towards the water, "Kevin!"

He didn't listen to her. Kalino came running over to see what had upset her so much.

"Becca! What's wrong?"

When she'd turned to look at him, his eyes went wide, and his face took on a furious expression. "Kalino! Go after him!"

"No! Dagan deserves whatever he gets. Kevin's going to kill him!"

"No! Dagan's heading out to the big waves! You know Kevin can't handle waves that big. Go get him. Please!"

Kalino immediately realized that Kevin wasn't thinking with anything other than the fury consuming him. He grabbed his board, and started paddling furiously after his best friend. He reached the first break point, and then watched in horror as Kevin kept going.

Dagan was already sitting on his board, waiting for the next big wave to form, and Kevin was headed straight for him.

"Oh no! Kevin!" He cupped his hands around his mouth, and yelled until he was hoarse, and then he watched in horror as the wave formed and Dagan paddled for it. Kevin wasn't in the right position to take on the monster wave, but he still kept going after Dagan.

The wave was the largest that Kalino had ever seen, more than fifty feet in height, and with a speed that had him fearing for his own safety some hundred yards away.

He watched as the wave started to break, and Dagan expertly entered the curl, but Kevin wasn't so lucky. He made it to an upright position, but the wave was breaking too fast for his inexperience. Kalino watched as the wave crashed down upon him, quickly obliterating both the boy and the board from site.

The wave didn't stop there though. It was Dagan's match, and before he could safely exit the tube, the wave took its second victim. Kalino paddled furiously towards where his friend had gone down, but another rogue wave came out of nowhere, lifting him and his board up, and sending him flying some twenty yards away.

He was the lucky one. Several other seasoned surfers had seen what happened and had already paddled out to lend a hand. Someone managed to pull him onto their board and take him back to the beach. They took him to the hospital, where he spent more than three weeks in a coma.

What followed was the stuff nightmares were made of. Two funerals. Two grieving parents who couldn't understand how she'd let this happen. One father who mourned his only child, even though he'd raised a daughter as his own since birth. One mother who'd taken one look at her disheveled and bruised daughter and thought the worst. One sister who was so consumed with guilt over Kevin's rage, she actually contemplated taking her own life a time or two.

But killing herself wouldn't bring Kevin back. It wouldn't restore her trust in guys, and it wouldn't heal the rift between her parents that seemed bigger than the Grand Canyon. Only time and distance could do that, so she'd made preparations to leave.

Becca waited around the islands until she was sure Kalino was going to pull through, and then she packed a bag and left. She didn't tell anyone where she was going, but her parents' house was like a tomb. No one spoke to her, and the guilt and remorse she felt for her part in Kevin's death was more than she could bear on a daily basis.

The surfers left and her parents quit taking future reservations. It was as if they themselves had died along with her brother. Every time her father saw her, his eyes grew cold, and he turned his face away from her. Her mother's looks of condemnation and judgment were even worse. In order to save herself, she needed to leave.

She left Hawai'i, her parents, and everything she'd known to make a new start for herself. Running as far away as Colorado had seemed like a good idea, and when she stepped off the plane on a cold wintry day, she prayed and hoped that one day she would be able to forget and move on with her life. One day maybe she could return to Hawai'i and reconcile with her parents and herself.

Chapter 1

Friday afternoon, the day after Thanksgiving Day, Denver, Colorado…

Jessica, Gracie, and Becca were standing in Adelaide's Bridal Shop, looking at a sea of wedding dresses. So far, Gracie had suggested several dresses for Jessica to try on, but none for herself.

Jessica was marrying Justin Donnelly, and Gracie had just become engaged to his younger brother Mason. Becca was just along for the ride, but she was having fun nonetheless. After a miscalculation on their recent hike to Maroon Peak, Becca had become temporarily stranded in Silver Springs, Colorado. Gracie had been her ride from Denver, but she'd injured her knee in a fall that had required surgery. She'd also gone and fallen in love with Mason Donnelly, a beau from her childhood.

They had announced that they were getting married, and Jessica and Justin had secretly confided they were headed down the aisle of matrimony themselves. Both girls had decided that a dress shopping excursion was in order.

After enjoying Thanksgiving Day at the Three Brother's Lodge, owned and operated by the three Donnelly brothers, Becca had ridden back to Denver with them. She was dreading going home to her small apartment, knowing that on the morrow Gracie would be returning to Silver Springs. Melanie had been her other roommate prior to her moving out a month earlier, but her husband had finally gotten his discharge papers from the military, and they were already headed to Florida to be with her family.

So here she was, helping the woman who was not only her best friend, but also her savior and counselor, pick out a wedding dress. The only problem was that Gracie couldn't seem to decide on anything today.

"Gracie?" Becca stood by her friend's elbow, hoping to help her get things started.

"Hey!" Gracie smiled at her, looking overwhelmed and a little out of sorts. She was normally very organized and together, but today, she was a little scattered. Becca chalked it up to the newness of being engaged, and knowing that her life was getting ready to change for the better.

"What kind of dress are you looking for?" Becca hadn't thought about marriage for herself since leaving Hawaii, and now that she was in the store, surrounded by yards of lace, satin, and sheer fabric, she wondered if she would ever be able to trust a man enough to make this type of commitment to him. She hoped so, but only time would tell.

Gracie sighed, "I don't know. I'm a lost cause today."

Becca smiled at her, "I doubt that. Tell me about the dress you wear in your dreams."

Gracie grinned, "But that is only a dream dress. And they don't really exist."

"Tell me anyway, okay?" Becca insisted. She knew Gracie had always dreamed of a wedding to her childhood beau, and now that her dream was getting ready to come true, she might as well have the dress to go with the rest.

"Velvet. In my dreams, my wedding dress is white velvet. It has a scoop neckline and lone sleeves with those little strings than hook over your middle finger to keep them in place. And a long skirt that swirls around my ankles when I walk, but drapes along the ground behind me."

"It sounds gorgeous. Tiffany, do you have anything like that?" Becca asked the store attendant Gracie hadn't known was standing behind her listening in.

Tiffany smiled, "I have the perfect dress for you. Head on back to the dressing room and I'll bring it to you."

Gracie looked at her, hope shining in her eyes, "You really have a dress like what I described?"

"Go on back and you'll see. It must have been made just for you." Tiffany turned to Becca and grinned, "This is weird, but she could have designed the dress I have hanging in back. It was sent here, by accident, from a European designer, and is a one of a kind. The shipping to send it back was going to be astronomical, so we decided to keep it."

Twenty minutes later, Gracie emerged from the dressing room, and everyone stopped and gasped at the picture she presented. She was stunning in the dress, and a more perfect fit didn't exist.

"Oh, Gracie! Look at yourself!" Jessica and Becca urged her.

Gracie took a breath, and turned to face the three-way mirror. She gasped and felt tears spring to her eyes. "It's perfect! Just like in my dreams."

Becca wrapped an arm around her waist, "Who was your perfect groom in your dreams?"

"Mason," Gracie whispered.

"A match made in heaven. She'll take it." Becca turned to Tiffany with tears stinging her own eyes. Gracie had been her saving grace more than once, and she was so happy for her friend, and yet – she knew she was going to miss her terribly when she returned to Silver Springs tomorrow. She fought back her tears, not wanting her own neediness to overshadow the day.

"Perfect." The store attendant was beaming as she walked away to start the paperwork.

"Now we have to find Jessica the perfect dress," Becca said.

"Well, I don't think I'm ever going to find anything as perfect as that one, but I have several to try on."

"Then get to it," Becca told her with a laugh.

An hour later, both girls had found the dresses of their wedding dreams, and they were heading back to Jessica's apartment. The same one she had shared with Becca and Melanie. They arrived to see the boys loading the last of the boxes into the trailer.

"All done?" Gracie asked in wonder, glancing at her watch.

"How about we go get some pizza?" Kaillar suggested, making sure that Becca knew she was invited as well. She liked Kaillar, and part of her wished she could get rid of her distrust and give him a chance. He was the middle Donnelly brother, and the most handsome in her opinion. He also seemed to like her. *You know better, he likes you – a lot. He's also hoping for – what she didn't know.*

While she was thinking about these things, plans were made to go get pizza from a place just a few blocks from the apartment, and Becca headed for Mason's car. She was halfway across the yard when her cell phone rang, stopping her in her tracks.

Upon leaving Hawaii, she hadn't changed her cell phone number. She'd kept it, even keeping the unique cell phone tones for her family members, hoping that one day her mother or father would call her and ask her to come home. It hadn't happened in four years. Until now.

With shaky hands, she turned and walked a short distance away. She pulled the phone from her pocket, and slid her thumb across the screen to answer the call, "Hello?"

"Becca?"

"Mom?" Becca asked, her voice going soft with disbelief. Her mother was calling her after all these years. *Why?*

"Becca, something horrible has happened."

Becca felt her heart crack a little more, the brittle pieces already in ruins. "What?" she whispered, closing her eyes as she willed the bad news away.

"Your father had a heart attack this morning. He's gone."

Becca heard her mother crying over the phone, and she felt her hand tremble. "What?" she asked incredulously.

"The funeral is Sunday. I'd like you to be here for the funeral."

Becca felt the world start to spin around her, dark spots forming in front of her eyes as she dropped the phone from lifeless fingers to the ground below. She tried to keep the darkness from taking her, but it rushed at her.

She moaned, and began to come around a few minutes later. Kaillar and Gracie were both peering down into her face, looks of concern on their faces. She looked around and realized that she was in the back seat of the car. She could hear Gracie's voice coming from the front seat. *What's going on?*

"Becca, you fainted. You're in the car with me. Who was on the phone?" It was Gracie speaking to her, softly and with compassion for her friend evident in her voice.

Becca stared straight ahead, "My mom."

"Your mom in Hawaii?" Gracie asked.

Becca nodded, "My dad's dead. The funeral is Sunday and she wants me there." She heard her voice, but it really didn't sound like her. The words she was speaking couldn't be coming from her

14

mouth, and yet – they were. Her father was dead, and her mother had called…

Gracie's wrapped her in a hug, "Oh Becca. I'm so sorry. Honey, what can we do?"

Becca wasn't crying. Not yet. "She wants me to come for the funeral. I…"

"If money is a problem, I can lend you as much as you need." Gracie was a problem solver, and she'd never met one she couldn't handle. Especially if the problem belonged to someone else. Gracie wanted everyone around her to be happy with life; it was one of the things that had originally drawn Becca to her. Gracie generally seemed happy, while Becca had been simply existing.

"No. I can…I just…," she looked up at Gracie with tears and fear in her eyes. "I can't go back there like this. Weak. I just can't. Not by myself. I…"

Becca felt horrible for even voicing her fears. She wasn't normally weak, but the recent assault had taken a greater toll on her psyche than even she wanted to admit. She saw Gracie's silent communication with Kaillar, and then he was speaking directly to her.

"Becca, darling. Do you want someone to go with you?" Kaillar had squatted down to peer into the vehicle, and she tried to meet his eyes and failed. *He deserves so much more than I can give him. But I don't want him to quit trying. I really don't.*

Becca's mind was almost numb, but she heard Kaillar talking to her and it sounded like he was offering her a lifeline. One she desperately needed right then. *Do I want someone to go with me? Yes, please!* She nodded her head, raising teary eyes to his own and watching them soften with compassion and something else she couldn't identify.

He laid a gentle hand on her shoulder and held her eyes, "I'll take you home. Will you let me do that? Will you let me take you home to say goodbye to your dad?"

Becca shivered once, but she didn't look away from him. "Yes."

"Good. Justin, we need a ride to the airport." Kaillar didn't hesitate and Becca sat there numbly, her mind replaying her mother's words over and over again. *He's gone. Her dad was dead.*

And just like that, Kaillar had stepped in and orchestrated everything. A quick trip by her apartment for clothing and toiletries. A quick shopping trip at a local clothing mall had yielded several outfits along with a small suitcase for Kaillar.

Then it was off to the airport where they caught a flight before dinnertime was over. Kaillar had stayed right by her side in the terminal, watching her carefully as if he expected her to breakdown any minute.

Becca purposefully shut her mind off. She thought of Gracie's last words to her, and she was amazed at the comfort they provided her. *Family. Family was more than just who you were biologically related to. Family was whomever you became attached to. People you would do anything for. People who stuck by you in the good times and the bad.*

Family was what she'd found in Colorado. *So what was she to do with the family she'd left behind in Hawaii?"*

Chapter 2

Saturday, Honolulu International Airport, Oahu, Hawaii ...

Becca Edwards watched the approaching tarmac with a sense of sadness so overwhelming that she wasn't sure if she would survive this trip home. So many memories...

She'd left the islands a little over four years ago. Four years that seemed like an eternity to her. She'd moved to the mountains of Colorado, figuring they were about as different from the lush tropical landscape of the Hawaiian Islands as she could get. She hadn't been wrong.

Mountains were the norm in Colorado, but unlike Hawaii where more often than not they were covered in cooled, or cooling lava, the mountains here were covered in snow for at least six months out of every year. She still remembered the first time she'd watched it snowing outside. The large flakes falling from the sky, so silently and peaceful looking.

She'd grabbed her camera and captured the moment. The first of many over the last four years. She'd always been interested in photography, and was a hobby writer, so majoring in photojournalism had seemed to be the perfect career choice for her once she landed in Denver. Becoming roommates and friends with Gracie and Melanie had also been perfect.

She'd been looking for a place to live, close to her classes, and Gracie and Melanie had been looking for a third roommate to help share their home and pay a third of the bills. The trio had hit it off from the very first, and Becca had thanked her lucky stars for meeting the two women who had helped her through one of the toughest times in her life. Even if they hadn't known what she was going through.

Everything in her life seemed to have been coming together, so much so that she'd stopped feeling so adrift on the sea of life. She'd seen some pictures taken by the Division of Wildlife personnel, and decided right then and there that was what she wanted to be doing. Getting out into nature and taking photographs that showed the beauty of life all around.

She'd still missed her family, but she'd not received one phone call from either of her parents since leaving Hawaii. She'd left them a letter, explaining that she couldn't live in a place surrounded by memories of what might have been, and that she was going somewhere to start over. She'd promised to come home when the time was right, but so far, thoughts of returning to Hawaii left her in a cold sweat. The only concession she'd made was once a year, a week before Christmas Day, she sent a postcard to let them know that she was still alive and not ready to come home yet.

She hadn't even chosen the postcard she was going to send this year, and now it seemed that she wouldn't be following that ritual for a fifth time. She rolled her head from side to side, trying not to let the questions of the past swamp her thinking.

What if her dad still felt the same way as he had when she'd left? What if her mother still had that look of condemnation in her eyes?

Either of those would have destroyed her, so she'd stayed away.

Not even after the assault had she considered calling or going home. She knew that Gracie and Melanie were both worried about her, but when she'd been grabbed in that parking garage, and the men had held her down, one with his hands around her throat, her brain had instantly reverted to the other time that had happened. And the horrible aftermath when her brother had found out what Dagan had done.

18

Her attackers had grabbed her from behind, muffling her screams for help. They'd dragged her off to a waiting car, where her nightmares had taken on new meaning. There had been three of them, all Hispanic and all speaking in what she thought sounded like Spanish.

They'd ripped her clothes, pinching and slapping her body to the point that she had feared for her life. One of them had produced a knife and tormented her by dragging the blade over her exposed body. He'd cared not that he'd broken the skin in several places, seeming to take great joy in the beads of blood left behind on the welts.

Becca had been sure she was going to die that night. But then, a security car had driven through the parking garage and had spooked her attackers. They'd kicked her to the garage floor and sped off. She'd been found moments later, and transferred by ambulance to the hospital. The nurses in the emergency room had all been very kind, and after treating her physical wounds, and ascertaining that her attackers had been disrupted before they could sexually assault her, they'd called in the resident shrink.

She'd been leery of trusting him, after her last mental health fiasco, but she'd also known that she needed to release the memories so they could start to fade. She'd told him everything that had happened and that had been said to her. After she'd finished, he'd wanted to know why she hadn't taken more steps to protect herself. After all, walking through a parking garage, at night, by herself, was practically begging someone to mistreat her.

His words had been so similar to the last counselor she'd sought out, a few weeks after arriving in Colorado, she'd felt like she was in a time warp.

Becca had kicked the hospital's psychologist out of her room and demanded that someone call her roommates to come and get her. When the nurses had asked her what was wrong, she'd refused to say a thing. She was done trusting people with her feelings and emotions.

Gracie had arrived fifteen minutes later, horrified that Becca had gone through such a trying ordeal and her roommates were just hearing about it. Becca hadn't told Gracie about the counselor, afraid she would say too much and leave an opening for her friends to start asking questions about the past as well.

It had been six months since her attack, and she still felt jumpy and nervous in dark places. Physically, she'd had some bruises and cuts, but mentally, it was as if her brain had been fire-stormed. Night terrors were just one of the ways her brain had chosen to deal with her attack. Panic attacks and an aversion to being touched were others.

Gracie seemed to think that she was suffering from a sort of PTDS, but Becca was adamantly against any kind of counseling. She'd tried that briefly after arriving in Colorado. The college medical center had a mental health doctor, and she'd gone to him exactly twice. The first time had been more of a meet and greet session.

But during the second session, the counselor had told her that she'd set herself up to be attacked by Dagan. He'd insinuated that she'd basically asked for what had happened and everything that had followed was in part her responsibility. He'd affirmed her guilt over her brother's death, reminding her that she was the one who made the decision to take off with her boyfriend. Her brother had paid for her lack of judgment.

She'd never gone back to another session, believing she could heap guilt on her own shoulders and didn't need to pay someone hundreds of dollars to help. Becca had slammed out of his office, recommending he find another vocation because his ability to listen without passing judgment was deplorable.

Coupled with her experience in the emergency room, Becca had no use for the entire counseling profession. Except for Gracie.

Gracie was a medical doctor, but she seemed to know more about how Becca's brain processed things than even Becca herself did. Without Gracie, she wasn't sure how she would have survived the last six months.

And yet, here she was heading to Hawaii without her. Gracie couldn't travel because of her knee surgery, so Kaillar had stepped in to provide the companionship and support she needed. For the first time in years, Becca could honestly say that she was glad to have a man's shoulder to lean upon.

Chapter 3

The plane's wheels touched down, and she felt her companion stir in the seat next to her. *Kaillar Donnelly.*

She glanced at him from the corner of her eye, watching as his lashes fluttered several times before opening and revealing his deep blue eyes beneath a mop of unruly dark blonde hair. He'd fallen asleep somewhere over the Pacific Ocean, and Becca had spent many long moments watching him sleep.

He was the middle brother of the three Donnelly men, and had offered to escort her home to say goodbye to her father. She'd tried to figure out why all of a sudden he had seemed to be safe to her, when only days earlier he'd sent tendrils of fear rushing through her body because he had stood too close to her.

Those feelings seemed to have vaporized and as he'd slept, she'd wanted nothing more than to lay her head on his shoulder and seek the same refuge in slumber. But Becca's dreams were more often than not unpleasant; and the fear that she would have a nightmare while trapped in this seat and on the plane had kept her awake the entire trip. A feat that even now was taking a great toll on her ability to function correctly.

Becca had never been the type of person who functioned well on just a few hours of sleep. She always felt as if she was wading through muddy waters, and that everyone was moving in slow motion around her the next day. She mentally groaned as she realized that by not sleeping, she'd possibly made a truly horrible day almost impossible to take. *I should have tried to get at least a few hours of sleep.*

But it was too late now. The flight was over. They'd flown from Denver to San Francisco and then taken a late flight off the mainland. It was now almost 10 a.m. on Saturday morning in Hawaii, but with the time difference, that meant Becca had been awake for almost thirty-two hours.

She looked back out the window, and called up the image of Kaillar she'd created in the wee hours of the morning. Yawning, she closed her eyes, and envisioned a beach with waves crashing off the shore as men and women tested their abilities against Mother Nature. It wasn't hard to imagine her companion in that setting. Coming across the sand in knee-length board shorts, his shoulders tan from many hours in the sun, the muscles rippling as he carried a surfboard on his shoulder. He'd use his free hand to sluice his too-long hair back and then stand the board up in the sand before walking towards her…

She'd participated in just such a scene many times, just with a different lead actor. The last time, the actor had been her beloved brother. She remembered the smile on his face dying as he got his first glimpse of her, and the angry way he'd grabbed his board and headed back to the ocean. It would be his last ride, and for that, she would never forgive herself.

The plane stopped moving as it docked at the terminal gate and Becca sighed. Most people came to Hawaii to vacation. But she and Kaillar weren't in Hawaii to play on the beach. In fact, she wasn't sure she wanted to play with the handsome man his friends referred to as Kai at all.

She'd first met him when she and her two friends had tried to climb Maroon Peak on the cusp of a major winter storm. Becca hadn't known the danger they were in, but she'd soon found out. The wind and snow had come upon them so quickly even now she found it miraculous that Gracie had been the only one hurt on their descent.

Kaillar and his brother Mason had come up the mountain to rescue them. Mason had gone after Gracie, and Kaillar had escorted her and Melanie to the small town of Silver Springs. Everything had been going fine until she'd slipped and Kaillar had reacted and caught her.

Even now, she felt horrible for how she had reacted. Gracie seemed to think she needed counseling to get past the attack that had happened not so long ago, but Becca felt sure she could conquer her own demons – she'd done so once before.

She'd never been one to confide in others, and most especially not matters of a personal nature. *Is that why you never sought any help with reconciling with your dad? It's too late now. Just like it was too late to save Kevin...*

Becca forced her thoughts away from that dark abyss, not willing to allow the past to torture her at this moment in time. The present was doing enough of that all on its own!

"Hey! We're here." Kaillar leaned towards her, craning his head to get a glimpse out the plane's small window.

"Very observant," came her flippant reply before she could stop it. She blushed and covered her mouth before sighing, "Sorry. Coming home..."

Kaillar sat back, pulled her hand away, and folded his long fingers around it, ignoring her small tug of protest. "I know this must be really hard for you. Gracie mentioned you hadn't been home in over four years?"

Becca looked at him, seeing the questions in his eyes, and then turned her head towards the window. "Yeah. Four years." She thought about leaving it there, but then she didn't want him assuming that she and her family were all nice and cozy. Once upon a time...

"Look, you should probably know that I've not even spoken to my family since I left Hawaii. Things were... difficult... when I left. My father...well, let's just say that not having to see me each day as a reminder of what he'd lost was a blessing."

"To him?"

She nodded, "Yeah. To him."

"And what about you? Was it a blessing being separated from your family for so many years?"

Becca looked at him and then shook her head once, "Yes, and no. But I'm not going to discuss that right now. I can't. I just wanted you to know that things may be a little tense when we reach my home."

He nodded once, and then pushed his arms forward as he stretched; an action that drew her eyes to the tight t-shirt he wore and how well it molded to his muscles. Realizing her brain was once again heading down a path that was only vaguely familiar to her, she forced herself to look away as she slowly gathered up her belongings from the seat in front of her.

"So, how far from the airport..."

"We have to grab a charter flight to the Big Island. This is only Honolulu." At his blank look, she smiled tightly, "Oahu. Where Pearl Harbor is?" When he nodded, she continued, "My family lives on the Big Island – Hawai'i."

"Okay. So, I didn't have Jessica grab us a charter flight..."

"Don't worry about it. Unless things have really changed around here, we shouldn't have any problem catching a flight."

"Does anyone know you're coming besides your mother?" Kai asked, the look on his face warning Becca that he would only take half answers for so long.

Becca gave him a rueful glance, "I'm not even sure I agreed to come home before passing out. I should probably call her, but I know she's got a lot on her plate right now." *And I don't know if I could handle it if she'd changed her mind and didn't really want me here. Better to just show up, and then deal with whatever outcome there was.*

The pilot turned off the fasten seatbelt sign and Becca felt her anxiety go up another notch. *Breathe in, Becca. You can do this. One. Two. Three. Breathe out. Good girl.* She could almost envision Gracie standing over her and counting as she went through the breathing exercises that had seen her through more than one panic attack. She opened her eyes, and tried to see the island as any other tourist would.

Hawaii was a place that people came to make beautiful memories. Until that fateful day four and a half years ago, she'd thought it was an idyllic place to grow up. Her parents owned a small upscale beach resort in Opihikao. It was more like an over-achieving bed and breakfast, and as far as she knew, her parents had still been running it upon her father's death.

Becca scooted to the aisle when it was her row's turn to disembark, and felt a small measure of thankfulness when Kaillar stepped back and waited for her to precede him from the plane. She nodded her thanks to the stewardess, and then stepped off the plane, immediately feeling a wave of homesickness as she breathed in the humid air that was like no other.

Fragrant flowers coated the air in a way only found on the islands, and the Hawaiian shirt clad greeter smiled broadly as she lifted a flower lei over Becca's head. "Aloha!"

"Mahalo," Becca offered softly in return, the syllables rolling off her tongue as if she'd not kept them locked away for years.

With her strawberry blonde hair and pale green eyes, she looked like any other tourist come to the islands for a bit of culture, some sand, and the chance to see a live volcano erupting. But Becca considered herself as much of a Hawaiian as the dark-skinned, dark-haired young men and women who could trace their Hawaiian heritage back for generations.

Becca's mother had come to the islands as a young adult, fresh out of high school. She'd fallen in love with a surfer, skipped returning home for the fall school semester to watch him train, and then compete during the winter months on the islands. An orphan, she didn't have any family to answer to, only herself.

When spring had arrived, the surfers had headed south and she'd been left behind. Four months pregnant with a baby on the way. A baby the father adamantly denied was his.

Her mother, Stacie, had refused to chase after him and had refused to name him on Becca's birth certificate. To this day, she didn't know who her biological father was, and had accepted that the secret would go to the grave with her mother. According to her, the man was already dead, and naming him now would serve no good purpose.

Becca had accepted that, and until tragedy had struck their family four years earlier, she'd never wanted to call anyone but the man who'd raised her – dad. She still didn't now, but words spoken from the midst of a broken and hurting heart couldn't be taken back, and she'd allowed them to fester now for four years.

She stepped further into the airport terminal, her mind continuing to think too hard about things she couldn't change. About the man she had lovingly called father all of her life. *Makoa Kahoalani.*

Three months after Becca was born, her mother had met the man when she took a job as a housekeeper at his family's resort. The two had fallen in love and when Becca was only six months old, they had been married in a traditional Hawaiian ceremony out behind the resort on the green grasses overlooking the ocean.

Her parents had been so happy, and she'd grown up knowing that she was loved. She and her brother...

Becca took a short breath, the pain of remembering making it almost impossible to face what she knew was going to be the hardest time in her life. She'd tried to mend her broken heart while living in Colorado, and it seemed that every time she thought she could see the light at the end of the tunnel, a new tragedy appeared in her life.

She'd been well on her way to healing before the attack in Colorado. Now, here she was, heading home to the place where all of her troubles had begun, to face yet another tragedy. And she was scared. Scared she wouldn't be able to handle the memories. Scared she'd run again. Scared she wouldn't recover this time.

Hearing Kaillar speaking to the greeter behind her, she turned and pasted a smile on her face that didn't even come close to reaching her eyes. She was in Oahu, and now she needed to face her past and find them a transport to the Big Island. So far, things had gone smoothly, but Becca was too pessimistic to imagine they would continue to be so.

This trip could very well destroy me. Again!

Chapter 4

Kaillar watched as Becca looked back at him, seeing the strain around her mouth, even though she was trying to smile for his benefit. He wanted to pull her into his arms and tell her that everything was going to be all right, but he didn't even know what everything was.

He'd tried to get her talking about her childhood, and she'd given him some facts, but nothing that would help him understood why she'd fled to the mainland to begin with.

Every time he even got close to asking a personal question, she'd changed the subject. He'd finally given up, and allowed himself to close his eyes and sleep. He'd hoped that she would do the same, but looking at the bruising beneath her eyes, he would guess that she hadn't slept for more than an hour since leaving Colorado the morning before.

"So, do we need to grab our luggage?" Kaillar asked, joining her, the flower lei around his neck almost overpowering, the fragrance was so strong.

"Luggage is downstairs. And yes, we do need to grab it." They hadn't brought much with them, this trip coming up suddenly and without notice. Becca had been able to pack hurriedly, but Kaillar only had a few changes of clothes with him, and his travelling toiletry bag. He'd assured her that he could purchase anything he needed once they reached their destination, and she hadn't argued with him. Because he was right.

The islands offered a plethora of shopping venues, and the Big Island was no different. Home to Kilauea, it was a popular destination for tourists wanting the complete Hawaiian experience.

The volcano had been erupting in one form or another ever since Becca could remember.

When it wasn't spewing forth molten lava and steam, slow moving lava tubes were creeping across the surface of the island, consuming anything in their path. A recent event had a small tube gradually moving towards Opihikao. So far, no homes had been destroyed, but Mother Nature and the volcano herself wouldn't be stopped before they were ready. If things continued to move in the same direction, her family's resort would barely make it to ring in the New Year before becoming yet another victim of the volcano.

She led him towards the escalators that would take them to the ground level and baggage claim areas. It would also give her an opportunity to see who had a charter flight heading back to the Big Island.

"Becca?" an incredulous voice grabbed her attention, making her swing her head around to confront a very rotund face from her past.

"Kalino?" Of all the people she'd expected to see at the airport, her brother's best friend wasn't even on the long list.

"Aloha! What are you doing here? The last time I spoke to your father…" The man broke off seeing the sadness on her face. "Oh no! What happened?"

Becca swallowed painfully, and then whispered, "He's dead."

Kalino watched her for a moment, glancing at her companion, before turning to her with a raised brow, "Did you speak to him before…"

She shook her head, wanting him to let the matter go. "My mother called…"

"When is the funeral? I would like to attend."

Becca's head was reeling, but Kalino's words registered, and she nodded. "He would have liked that. I believe it's tomorrow. We just arrived from the mainland, and I need to find us a ride."

"Done! I don't have any other fares scheduled for today or tomorrow. I was going to head to Maui, and get some practice rides in before the competition starts next weekend."

"Competition?" Kaillar asked, stepping in behind Becca and wondering who this man talking with them was.

"Surfing. Kalino is one of the best." Becca looked between the two men, wondering what was going through Kaillar's head. She was hoping she wouldn't have to explain her comment or how she knew it to be true. She might have left Hawaii, but she'd secretly followed Kalino's career as a world class surfer, and she only hoped he turned out better than Dagan had. Fame and popularity could be anyone's downfall, and having scores of scantily clad women throwing themselves at you all the time, telling you how wonderful they think you are, was enough to make even the strongest man of integrity think with his ego instead of his mind and heart.

She would be heartsick if that ever happened to Kalino, and part of her was silently rejoicing at the evidence in front of her to the contrary. Kalino was barely nineteen, and other than growing in stature and the deepening of his voice, he seemed much the same as before. Before he'd lost his best friend and her world had come crashing down about her ears. *Kevin would have been the same. If only...*

It was as if Kalino had picked up her train of thought. He searched her eyes for a moment before turning to Kaillar and shaking his head. "No. A close second. Kevin was the best," he murmured to her softly.

Becca looked at him sadly and shook her head, "Please. Don't go there. This is hard enough."

31

Kalino sighed in frustration, "You leaving was hard." Becca merely shrugged, as if her agreement mattered not. "Look, why don't you all grab your luggage and meet me at the charter desk in half an hour? I'll go file a new flight plan, and we'll head out right after that."

"Thank you."

"Don't mention it." He looked at her companion, and Becca realized she'd yet to make any introductions.

"Sorry," she mumbled to both men. "Kalino, this is Kaillar Donnelly. Kai, this is Kalino. He was a friend of my brother's."

Kalino gave her a strange look, which she ignored. He'd been more like a brother to her growing up, and something told her he could be again, if she could just get past her own guilt.

"Nice to meet you." Kaillar shook his hand, and then placed a gentle hand on her lower back, "We really appreciate your offer of a ride. This has been hard on her, and anything you can do to make things easier is welcome and appreciated."

"*A`ole pilikia.* See you both soon." Kalino strode off, and Becca released a breath she hadn't even known she was holding. She'd known that she would see people from her past, but seeing he brother's best friend right off the bat had been more than merely hard. *Guess you no longer have to wonder if seeing people you once knew was going to send you running off.*

Becca glanced at Kaillar, and then interpreted for him, "He just told us not to worry, and that's all."

Kaillar nodded his head, and then directed her with light pressure on her back towards the sign indicating the baggage claim was still ahead of them. They had to navigate several large groups of people who seemed to be enthralled with the airport, wanting to document their arrival in Hawaii with photos from every angle.

Becca wished that she could tell them they needed to step outside if they truly wanted to experience their first moment in Hawaii, but then again, that would require interacting with strangers. Something she rarely did unless forced to.

"So, I didn't know you have a brother," Kaillar offered once they were moving toward the baggage claim again.

Becca nodded once, "Yeah. I did have a brother."

"Had? What happened?" he wondered aloud.

"He died. Can we change the subject?" she asked through tightly clenched lips.

"Sure." Kaillar watched her for a moment, knowing that whatever she was hiding more than likely wasn't going to stay hidden while she was here. How could it? The past always had a way of catching up with you and forcing you to deal with it. The only question that remained was whether you would choose the how and when, or find yourself being thrown into the chaos, struggling to find an anchor to hold on to.

Kaillar hoped for Becca's sake that she took control of the situation and dealt with her past on her terms when she was ready and strong enough to deal with them. When she was strong enough to handle whatever the past might entail. Whatever the case may be, Kaillar mentally promised her to stay by her side and provide whatever support she needed in the coming days. It was what he wanted to do. Help her.

Chapter 5

He was prevented from thinking more about the subject as the baggage carousel starting moving and their bags appeared a few moments later. "Now where do we go?"

Becca relaxed a bit, acknowledging that he was willing to stop his questioning for the moment. "This way."

"So, how long of a flight is it over to the Big Island?"

"Not long. Kalino and his family operate a charter service, so their planes aren't commercial grade nor do they carry many passengers. When I left, their largest plane could only carry up to ten passengers."

"Must have been nice to know someone growing up who could shuttle you around to the various islands. Did you do that often?"

Becca nodded her head, "All the time. Kalino's dad was always offering to let us kids tag along."

"So which of the islands is your favorite?" Kaillar asked.

Becca smiled, "That's easy. Molokai." She smiled as she remembered the island's many valleys and waterfalls. It was a beautiful island, the hillsides brilliant green as they rose up from the ocean's floor.

"Maybe we'll have time for you to show it to me before we go home?" Kai suggested, liking the smile that had flitted over her face for just a moment.

Becca nodded her head, "Maybe. That might be fun." Molokai only held good memories for her, so a trip there would be most welcome.

They took the escalator back up, and she led them through the various shops hawking their souvenirs to the unsuspecting tourists who had waited too long to pick up that last memento of their time on the islands. They would pay almost double the cost for t-shirts, sweatshirts, and postcards, but they would smile while doing it, and everyone would be happy.

"Tourism is big here," Kaillar commented, having noticed the plethora of shops himself.

Becca nodded, "Yeah, it doesn't seem to have improved any while I was away. The Big Island is slightly better, unless you are in the larger areas of the city or the commercial beaches."

"Commercial beaches?" Kaillar asked. He'd been to California a time or two, but the beaches there mostly belonged to the State of California and were managed like State Parks.

"There are quite a number of private beaches in Hawaii. It's possible to not only purchase the dry land, but a large portion of the ocean front. In addition, you have different types of beaches here. There are the traditional white sand beaches, but also some gorgeous black sand ones as well."

"Black sand beaches? Never heard of such a thing." He directed them towards a small coffee shop, continuing their conversation while they waited in line. "What makes the sand black?"

Becca smiled, "It's not really sand, not like you would typically define it. Rather, its cooled lava that has been weathered by the waves until it has been broken down into small particles that cover up the beach. There are good things and bad things about those beaches."

"What's the good?"

"The black sand particles are larger, and don't tend to stick to everything quite as readily."

"That sounds like a good thing, although I don't imagine building sand castles works well."

Becca laughed softly, "Not at all, as a matter of fact."

"What's the bad?"

"The bad comes when you go into the water. The icy cold water. It tends to numb one's feet up, so they don't immediately realize their treading upon very sharp, very ragged cooled lava. The farther out one goes, the less weathered the ocean floor becomes. It's like walking around on shards of broken glass.

"Most people don't realize what's happening to their bare feet until they return to the beach and as their body temperature returns to normal, so does their blood flow. They find themselves on the beach with stinging, hurting feet that are bloody and covered in small cuts and punctures."

"Ouch! Why don't they warn people?"

"Oh, they do. Most of those beaches have signs advising people to not enter the water without water shoes on their feet or dive socks in place. But tourists tend to think they know best and many of them don't come prepared. The worst part is after they go back home to wherever they're from."

"How's that?" Kaillar asked, giving the barista their orders and then paying for them before Becca could protest.

"The cooled lava provides a great breeding ground for coral and other microorganisms to hang out. If they don't properly clean their cuts, they get back to the mainland with injuries that continue to get infected and won't heal. Most of the bigger resorts and hotels have onsite medical stations to help educate and treat people who have injured themselves by not reading the warning signs."

"Sounds like it would behoove people to have someone knowledgeable about the island with them."

"It does help. Hawaii is a beautiful place, but also very dangerous. Even deadly."

Kaillar handed her the cup of coffee, and then led her over to a railing that looked down upon the terminal below. "You know firsthand about that." It was a statement, not a question.

Becca sipped her coffee and nodded sadly, "Yeah. I do."

"Will you tell me about it? Not right this minute," he told her when she started to deny him with a shake of her head. "Just…sometime while we're here, will you talk to me about what happened? Something tells me you haven't done that with many people."

Becca looked down and murmured, "No one actually." She looked up at him, her eyes growing slightly watery and she cleared her throat, "People think they know what happened that day, but no one truly does. Not that's still alive to talk about it. They all just assumed…," she cleared her throat again. "I haven't talked to anyone about that day."

"Why not?" Kaillar asked softly, amazement in his voice.

"What difference would it have truly made? The only people that mattered thought I was guilty, and I am. Just not for the reasons they believe. But the reasons don't change the fact that because of me, and my actions, my brother is dead."

"You might be surprised at how …."

"No. Nothing will ever make this better." She glanced up, and saw Kalino standing by the charter desk, waving to them. "Looks like he's ready to go."

Kai watched her carefully for a moment and then nodded, as if he'd agreed to her silent request to change the subject. He stepped up close to her, searching her eyes for some hidden answer, "You don't sound all that thrilled about going home."

"No."

When she didn't elaborate, he touched her shoulder, "Becca, if there's anything I can do…"

"There's not. I mean, having you here is helping already." When he continued to look at her in grave concern, she attempted a smile, "I'm fine. Tired. Hungry. And in need of a shower, but I'll be fine. Stop looking so worried."

"I wish there was something I could do to make this easier for you," he murmured. "Gracie would probably…"

"Gracie would be too emotional and trust me, that's not what I need right now." *I thought I wanted Gracie with me, but she would force me to deal with the emotions, and I'd be a bawling mess by now, and probably for the rest of my stay. I need to be strong, get through the funeral, and then get back to Colorado where I can bury all of these useless emotions once again.*

Chapter 6

She finished walking across the tiled terminal floor to meet Kalino, offering him up a forced smile. She could see the worry and questions in his eyes, but after dealing with Kaillar's questions, she didn't have anything left in her defenses. She sent a silent plea up that he would leave things alone.

"You all ready to fly?" Kalino asked with a big smile, seeing the worry on Becca's face, and knowing she was afraid he was going to force her to talk about the past. He wasn't sure what she'd been doing for the last four years, but dealing with the past didn't seem to be one of them.

He owed it to Kevin to help his sister while she was here, but not right now. She looked exhausted and he could see she was teetering on the edge of losing control. He'd be patient and when the time was right, he'd do what he could to help her heal. But he couldn't let her think that he didn't care. That he hadn't thought about her and wondered how she was doing. He had to at least let her know that much before they flew home.

Becca nodded her head, "Ready as I've ever been."

Kalino's eyes clouded at the trepidation he heard in her voice. He met her just before she went through the doorway, lowering his voice, "Becca, I never got a chance to say how sorry I was about Kevin. Things were so crazy, and I…"

Becca shook her head at him, "You were in a coma. I waited to leave until I knew you were going to be all right, but I couldn't stay any longer. It was just too hard."

Kalino nodded, "It took me a long time before I could go back out on a board. I still think about him every time I do."

Becca felt tears sting her eyes, and she wiped them away with a hand, "Thanks for being his friend. He was happiest when he was with you out on the water." She took a deep breath, and then stood up a little taller, "I'm ready to go home."

"Then let's do this thing." Kalino gave Kaillar a nod of his head, and then he led the way out to his twin engine, fixed prop, Cessna plane with the bright hibiscus flower painted on the side.

"Nice ride," Kaillar commented, ducking his head as he climbed into the seating area behind Becca. With her diminutive figure, she'd had no trouble entering the small aircraft, but his height wasn't nearly as kind. At 6'6" tall, he was always having to watch bumping his head in places others didn't. The plane presented a new problem, in that he couldn't stand up completely even once he cleared the doors.

He quickly chose a seat directly across from Becca, glad for the opportunity to sit, rather than stoop.

"Not much head room back there, sorry," Kalino called from where he sat in the pilot's seat.

"No worries," Kaillar assured him. His phone buzzed, and he quickly turned it off.

"One of your brothers?" Becca asked.

"Yeah. Justin's called twice now, wanting to make sure we arrived safely and to see how you're doing." He looked at her, and then lowered his voice, "What do I answer?"

"About how I'm doing?" she asked, waiting for his nod before she thought for a moment. "Well, I'm sure he's only asking because the girls are. Tell him I'm fine and that we should be back in a couple of days."

A couple of days? "Really? You don't want to stick around and help your mom?"

Becca turned her head to the window and shrugged, "I doubt she would want my help. Things between us weren't good when I left."

Kaillar was quiet for a moment and then asked, "Is this about your brother?"

"Partially. So many things happened at the same time, and my mother was grieving. We all were, but I think my brother's death hit her harder than the rest of us." She shook her head, "I'd rather not dredge all that up again."

Kaillar nodded his head, "I'm here if you need to talk. Why don't you tell me about this resort you grew up on?"

Becca nodded; taking the opportunity he was giving her to change the subject. "Well, it started out as a large beach house and over the years, my grandparents built additional bungalow style living units on the property. At one point in time, it was a pineapple farm, but they discovered there was much more money to be made catering to tourists than there was in growing pineapples."

"Are your grandparents still alive?"

"No. They both died when I was little. My grandmother passed first, when I was in the fifth grade. It was the first funeral I'd ever gone to, and I was a little mystified that everyone seemed so happy. I remember sitting up in the trees watching everyone eat and laugh, wondering why no one was crying. I felt like crying."

"Funerals are tough on kids," Kaillar commented.

"Yeah. Anyway, my mom found me and explained to me that sadness served no purpose. It wouldn't bring them back, and it only made getting on with living harder. I believed her, and when my grandfather passed away a few years later, I joined in the festivities and tried not to feel sad."

"But you were?"

"I was. My dad was too. He hid it well, but I would find him sometimes late at night, standing in the backyard with tears streaming down his face. He never knew I saw him, and he always composed himself before he came back inside."

"Crying wasn't acceptable to your father?" Kaillar asked, wondering if she'd learned to hide her emotions from him.

"Not to a man. I think that's why my brother and he fought so often. My father spent his entire adult life hiding his emotions away from the world, while my brother wore his heart on his sleeve for all to see."

Kalino had been listening to the conversation and interjected, "Kevin was the coolest kid in school. Smart. Athletic. Good looking. All of the guys were jealous of him."

Kaillar asked, "He was younger than you?" When she nodded, he asked, "By how much?"

"Five years. Mom had a couple of miscarriages, and she always said Kevin was her miracle baby."

"What did she say about you?" Kaillar wanted to know.

Becca looked at him and then away, mumbling, "I'm the one who broke her heart."

Kalino heard her, turned his head, and shook it, "You know that's not entirely true. Your mom doted on you. Whatever you think you know, remember you left before anyone had time to heal. Your mom was grieving and continued to do so, not only for Kevin, but because you'd left."

Becca stared at him, "That's not true. They were glad when I left. They didn't have the constant reminder of how much I'd cost them."

Kalino made an angry sound, and then faced front again, "If I weren't flying this plane, I'd shake you for saying something so stupid. Your parents loved you, and Kevin, so much."

Becca fell silent, Kalino's threat sliding off her shoulders as if it had never been uttered. She wasn't afraid of him, but he seemed very angry over her perception of things.

Kaillar wasn't quite so ready to let the subject drop. He felt the conversation needed to continue, so he pressed, "What's he talking about?"

"Remember that whole, I don't want to talk about this right now, conversation we had just a few short minutes ago?" When he nodded, she continued, "That's what he's talking about."

"The conversation you never had with anyone." He stated it as fact, not a question.

Becca sighed, "Yeah. That one."

Kaillar looked at her, and then spoke to Kalino, "Do you know what happened?" He tried not to notice the look of defeat on Becca's face. He needed to know what he was walking into, and since she wouldn't tell him, he'd ask someone else. Someone who seemed to be intimately acquainted with the entire situation. Whatever the situation was.

Chapter 7

Kalino looked at him and asked, "The day her brother died?"

Kaillar nodded, "I think that's the day I'm talking about. The day that she isn't."

Kalino gave Becca a sad look. An apologetic look that said he was sorry, "You let them all believe the worst, didn't you?" He was remembering the bruising on her cheek and around her throat. No doubt, she had allowed them to assume the worst. "Tell me you didn't protect him," he demanded, even this many years later, he was not willing to give Dagan a pass on his deplorable behavior.

"I didn't have to, no one asked. They automatically assumed." She answered him woodenly, her gaze fixed out the small window.

"What, that you'd let him have his way with you? How did you explain the bruises around your throat?" Kalino demanded, trying to calm down so he didn't crash them into the ocean below. The emotions of that day were bubbling up, and he strove to keep them in perspective. Something Becca obviously hadn't done.

"My mom was the only one who seemed to notice them, and her looks said it all. Whatever had happened was entirely my fault, and mine alone. She'd warned me about Dagan…"

"Wait a minute!" Kaillar interjected, his mind scrambling to keep up with the conversation. He turned to Becca and demanded with his eyes and his voice, "Bruises around your throat?"

"It's not what you think…," she tried to calm him down, looking at him with a haunted look in her eyes that was a knife to his heart.

"That's good, because I'm thinking this Dagan character deserved to be beaten to a pulp."

"The ocean did that for you. Thanks," Becca told him sarcastically before turning her head away once again. She was tired of this conversation, because it was getting nowhere. The facts didn't change the outcome. Her brother had blamed Dagan for her condition, and gone after him. She'd not been able to stop him, and both of them had lost their lives.

Kaillar watched her shields come up, and mentally kicked himself. Kalino met his eyes briefly, and then began to tell him about that day's tragic events. By the time he was finished telling the story, Becca had tears running down her face, and Kalino was speaking to the tower at the Hilo airport in preparation for landing.

Kaillar reached over and grabbed her hand, holding on tight when she tried to tug it away. "Shush. Becca, I don't know what's been going through your head, but as soon as we can, you need to call Gracie and talk with her about this. You've been hiding for four years from something that should have been dealt with immediately. I'm sorry that the people in your life let you down."

Becca took a shuddery breath as she struggled for control, "No, you have it all wrong." She looked at him, and the sadness in her eyes broke his heart. "I let them down. I was older, and should have taken steps to protect Kevin. I should have never gone down to the beach. He was only fourteen and…"

"It doesn't matter. You should have had someone in your life you could talk to about what Dagan did. He hurt you, and if you never say what happened, he gets away with it."

"He's dead! He's not getting away with anything!" she insisted.

Kaillar shook his head, "That's where you're wrong. If you don't explain what happened, at least to one person, he does get away with it. In your own mind, he gets away with it because it's a secret you have to keep locked away; along with all of the bitterness and pain it brought to your life."

Becca shook her head, "I tried that. The counselor was kind enough to affirm that my guilt was right where it belonged. I'd acted without a care for my own well-being, leading Dagan on, and the aftermath of that decision cost my brother his life."

Kalino was furious that anyone would dare to let her believe that the events of four years ago were her fault. She was the victim! But he couldn't have this conversation with her, because the tower was responding and they were getting ready to land.

He clenched his jaw for a moment, and then let out a breath, "We're landing. Hang on," Kalino called from the cockpit.

Becca was grateful for the interruption, but as they landed and retrieved their luggage, Kaillar's words kept replaying in her mind. *Had she really let Dagan off the hook by not telling anyone what had really happened? In effect, she'd protected his memory from being tainted by his horrible actions. She'd saved others from having to face the reality that their friend and family member wasn't honorable or the cool guy they'd idolized. He was an abuser, and she had no doubt in her mind that if the park ranger hadn't arrived when he did, he would have been able to add rapist to his list of crimes.*

Kaillar watched her, as did Kalino, but neither of them said anything more on the subject. She was left to muddle through her own thoughts; trying to make sense of what was real and what was the result of hiding the truth for so long. *Would speaking the truth to someone about that day be what she needed to finally heal? Someone who wasn't there to judge her, but just listen and possibly, maybe...agree that she'd been the victim? Kaillar and Kalino thought that way. Well, they sounded as if they thought that way, but then again, they didn't know all the facts. They didn't know that she'd willingly gone with Dagan. That would change everything.*

She had no doubt in her mind that Gracie would feel the same way. Gracie had told her time and again that the attack in the parking garage wasn't her fault. That she was the victim. But the counselor... Who was right?

She wanted to move on with her life so badly, but she'd only ever made it so far. *Maybe Kaillar was right, and she needed to call Gracie and confide in her.* She couldn't confide in either Kalino or Kaillar. It wasn't because she didn't think they would understand, it was simply her own fear of judgment from that quarter. She didn't think it would make things any worse, but she was beginning to really like Kaillar, and didn't want to jeopardize that by showing him how stupid she'd been.

If she was going to put herself back out there and risk judgment again, she'd choose the source she was almost positive would be supportive. She couldn't trust a stranger to do that. Not again.

No, she'd talk to Gracie, and that would be the end of it. She wasn't sure when that would happen, but if today was any indication, she needed to make the call sooner than later.

"So, you two want a ride to Opihikao?" Kalino asked after following them into the terminal.

Becca shook her head, "No. We'll take a taxi out. Thanks for the lift." Kalino had told her that he lived on the opposite side of Hilo, and she didn't want to take him any further out of his way.

"You don't have to thank me," Kalino told her, pulling her close for a hug before releasing her. "*E komo mai.* Welcome home, sister. Welcome home."

"Thanks. Come by later. I'm sure mom will be happy to see you."

"I will. Kaillar, it was good to meet you. Take care of her, and don't let her take too much on those tiny shoulders. Guilt is a horrible thing to wrap around one's neck. Just remember that, Becca."

She walked away, stepping out of the terminal to hail the first cab she could find. She was done discussing the past, and trying to focus on the difficult task that lie before her. Hopefully, the community had gathered around her mother to make the funeral preparations easier. There would be a burial ceremony, but the feast and party afterwards would be the hardest for both of them to bear. Becca didn't want to hear the drums beating happily along, or hear the people laughing as they danced and ate the food so soon after he father's body had been placed in the ground. She understood about celebrating a person's life, but somehow she would much prefer a more quiet remembrance than a party type of atmosphere.

She knew without asking that his body would not be cremated. He came from a very staunch Hawaiian ancestry that believed the bones of a human carried with them divine power. To cremate them would be to disrespect that power and intolerable. His body would be carefully preserved, and placed in a casket before being buried in a traditional gravesite.

While some Hawaiians would have a burial at sea, she knew her mother would never allow that. The sea had already claimed her son; she wouldn't willingly give it her husband as well.

Becca might have been gone for four years, but she still knew her mother. And that was part of the problem. Her mother had always been opinionated, and the last few weeks before the tragedy, she'd been short tempered with Becca's insistence on following Dagan around. She'd warned her daughter that the man was nothing but trouble, and she'd been right. Becca should have listened to her.

Chapter 8

"Becca?" Kaillar touched her on the shoulder, bringing her back to the present.

She blinked, and then realized a taxi was parked directly in front of her, the back passenger door open and awaiting her arrival. "Sorry. I guess I got sidetracked."

She slipped into the taxi, and gave the driver the address to the resort. She watched out the window as the vehicle made its way out of the airport and began the drive along the coastal road. When she began seeing the warning signs about the slow moving lava tubes, she couldn't resist asking, "How close are they to the location I gave you?"

"About two miles, miss. They have everyone on standby alert, but I wouldn't worry while you're here. The tube hasn't really moved much in the last month or so."

"Really? That's good news." Becca breathed a sigh of relief. She'd seen the coverage on the national news, and she'd been relieved when they'd put up the map and she'd realized her childhood home wasn't in the direct path of destruction.

"It is," the driver agreed. "My family's home is in the evacuation zone, and we've already moved my grandmother to another place, and removed the furniture and keepsakes."

"I'm sorry," Becca told him.

"No, do not be sorry. It is as my grandmother say. This land was birthed from the volcanoes, and eventually everything circles back to its origin."

"Dust to dust," Becca nodded her head.

"Yes."

"Lava tubes? Are we talking about molten rock here?" Kaillar asked.

Becca smiled at him, glad for something to talk about that didn't include her family or the past. "There are three main volcanoes on the island. Kilauea is the smallest of the three now…"

"Now?" Kaillar asked.

"Yes. She blew her top back in the 80's, and is only about four thousand feet above sea level right now. The other two mountains you saw as we flew around the island were Mauna loa and Mauna kea. They are both just short of fourteen thousand feet, but neither of them are really active. Mauna loa erupted back in the 80's as well, but doesn't seem to have much activity since then. Kilauea is a different story. She hasn't ever stopped erupting, and the crater rises and falls over time."

"When you say erupting, you mean like explosions and such?" Kaillar asked.

"Sometimes," Becca offered him a small smile, and then she looked out the window and her smile broadened. "We're here."

Kaillar looked out the window, and saw what looked like a little piece of paradise. A large two story building with wrap around porches on both levels stood behind a large expanse of green foliage and grass. Palm trees, flowering hedges, and a plethora of large leafed plants bordered the property.

To the side of the main house, small bungalows were connected by a covered walkway, painted white and enclosed here and there with lattice boards.

"You grew up here?" Kaillar asked, thinking that it looked like something one would see on a postcard.

"I did," she told him, watching him and liking the joy she saw on his face. That was something she'd noticed about Kaillar, his ability to take joy in his surroundings. If was infectious, and more than once since meeting him, she'd been jealous of his ability to enjoy his life. That was what she wanted most – to just enjoy being alive and not feel as if she didn't have the right to do so.

"It's absolutely gorgeous."

Becca nodded, but before she could reply, her attention became focused on the small woman with the graying hair who had come out of the house to greet her visitors. Becca knew the exact moment her mother recognized her. She tossed down the dishtowel in her hands, and started crying even as she ran towards Becca.

Becca felt tears start, and was helpless to stop them as she met her mother in the middle of the yard and felt those slim arms surround her for the first time in over four years.

"Becca! My sweet girl! Welcome home!"

Becca held her mom close, the feeling of being held in her mother's arms one that completely broke down the rest of her defenses. She held on, sobs coming from a place deep within her. Her mother simply held her and cried with her.

Becca had no idea how long they stood there on the grass, but she sensed Kaillar behind her, and slowly pulled away from her mother. Not sure what to say regarding what had just taken place, she opted for making her introductions.

She wiped her cheeks, and then stepped back so that her mother could see Kaillar, "Mom, this is Kaillar Donnelly. Kai, my mother, Stacie Kahoalani."

Kai stepped forward and shook her mother's hand, "Ma'am. Your place here is amazing!"

Stacie offered him a soft smile, "This is your first trip to the islands?"

"Yes, ma'am." Kaillar's smile was easy, and compassion shown in his eyes when he took her mother's hand in his own and softly told her, "I'm very sorry about your husband."

"Thank you." Stacie looked between the handsome man and her daughter, and then she stepped back, "Come inside."

Becca had seen the speculative look in her mother's eyes, and knew that at some point her mother was going to want answers about…everything. After her crying jag, her eyes felt puffy, and her throat was clogged with unshed tears. But she felt better. Almost as if the load she carried was lighter.

Stacie led them into the main house, leading them directly to the large sitting room at the rear of the property. It overlooked a private salt water pool and a large patio where guests were welcome to barbecue and enjoy the sunshine away from the crowded beaches.

"I'm so glad you came. When I didn't hear back from you, I got worried," her mother told her.

Becca started to answer, but Kaillar came to her rescue. "I'm afraid that's my fault. Your news was so shocking to Becca she fainted. Once her friends and I figured out what had happened, it was only a matter of a few hours before we were boarding a plane in Denver…"

"Denver?" Stacie asked, turning to look at her daughter. "Is that where you've been these many years? I saw the postmark on your yearly cards, but the town never made much sense to me." Seeing Kaillar's confusion, she explained, "Becca has sent a post card every year just before Christmas, but it was always postmarked North Pole. Her father and I were afraid she'd moved to the top of the world."

Kaillar smiled and then asked Becca, "You drove to the North Pole to mail your cards?"

Becca nodded her head, "It wasn't much of a drive, and I actually enjoyed being there every year during the holidays."

Becca turned to her mother, "Yes. I've been living in Colorado. North Pole is a small town about an hour's drive from Denver." She paused and then added, "I just finished college."

Stacie smiled at her daughter, "Your father would have been so happy to hear that. He..." She paused, glancing at Kaillar, uncomfortable with discussing family issues without knowing his connection to her daughter.

"It's okay mom. Kaillar knows what happened."

"Does he?" her mother asked with a raised brow. "Then maybe you could fill me in as well."

Becca shook her head, "You know what happened. You were there..."

Her mother was quiet for a moment and then sighed, "I saw what you wanted me to see."

Becca hadn't a response, and finally she changed the subject. "What do you need me to do for tomorrow?"

"Nothing. Everything's already been taken care of. Your presence is all that is required."

"Fine. Dress?"

"Traditional white. Did you..."

"I brought something appropriate with me. I'm going to go get Kai and myself settled. Any guests?"

"No. Julia cancelled everyone's reservations for me," she offered, referring to the older woman who helped her mother manage the cooking and cleaning tasks for the guest rooms. Julia was about the same age as her mother, and had been a figure in Becca's life for as long as she could remember.

"I'm glad Julia's still helping you out." She didn't wait for her mother to say anything else; she stood up and headed for where Kaillar had stacked their bags by the door. "Ready?"

Kai nodded his head, giving her mother a brief smile, and then followed her from the house, both bags in his hands. "You doing okay?"

"No. I just needed...I need to talk to Gracie." Becca sniffed as she led him down the covered walkway towards the standalone bungalows.

"Where are we going?" Kai asked as she passed several without stopping.

"The end. I just need some distance..."

"Becca?" When she turned and looked at him over her shoulder, he shook his head at her, "Stop!"

She did, and then crossed her arms protectively over her chest, "What?"

"Are there no guest rooms in the main house?"

She nodded once, "Yes."

"Then why aren't we staying there? Close to your mom?"

She watched him for a moment and then looked up, blinking her eyes furiously as she tried not to cry. "I just need some space."

"Fine. Then let's drop these bags off and take a drive. But you came home to say farewell to your father and if I'm not mistaken, reconcile things with your mother before you no longer could. Am I right?"

She nodded once, and then wiped a tear away with her fingertips.

"Then it's my job as your escort to see that you do that. To save you from making a mistake that you will most certainly regret. Let's go back to the main house, and then you can show me your island. Yes?"

She took a steadying breath, and then reversed course. She entered the main house from a side door this time, and led him up a flight of stairs. She stopped at the top, and pushed open the first door they came to. "You can use this room. It has its own bathroom through that door."

"This will be fine. Where are you going to stay?"

"My old room. The only other room was my brother's, and I just…"

"Don't say any more. Go make your call to Gracie, and then come find me. I'm going to call Justin, and make sure he doesn't call out the cavalry."

Becca found that mildly funny, "No cavalry here. Fly boys, yes. Sea dogs, most certainly. But no cavalry. You're in Hawaii now."

Kaillar gave her a small smile, and then nodded towards the door, "Go take care of things." He waited until she left before blowing out a breath. Since arriving at her childhood home, things had been a rollercoaster of emotion, and he was afraid that there was much more to come. He only hoped she could handle it, and that he'd have big enough shoulders to help.

H placed his call to Justin and at the end of the call, he asked his brother to call Pastor Jeremy and get the prayer chain going. Becca needed help, and after speaking with Justin for a few minutes, he realized that while he could offer her his support and be there to listen, ultimately she was going to have to deal with the emotional trauma that had been festering for way too long. He only knew one person who could help her through that, he only hoped when the time came, she was open to seeking help from a higher power.

Chapter 9

Becca entered her childhood bedroom, shocked to see that it was just as she'd left it. She walked around the room, looking at the pictures and posters hung on the walls as memories assailed her of happier times. When she reached the window, she pulled the blinds open, and was saddened to see that her view of the ocean was no longer there. The palm trees planted at the edge of the yard had grown up and now blocked her view.

She turned away from the window, and approached her desk and the small hutch that stood atop it. There were pictures of her and Kevin there. A picture of Kevin holding his trophy after winning a surf competition. Kalino and he had tied for the win, and another picture stood on the opposite side of the hutch of Kalino in a similar pose, holding an identical trophy.

She reached for the picture, and that's when she realized there was no dust. None. She looked around the room, and could tell that someone had been cleaning the room on a regular basis. She walked to the closet, finding the clothing she'd left behind hanging neatly from the rod.

The bureau, likewise, was just as she'd left it. Her clothing from four years earlier still neatly folded and awaiting her return. It was as if the room had been suspended in time!

Before she could dwell on that too much, her cell phone rang, and she pulled it from her pocket. One glance at the screen told her Gracie had gotten tired of waiting for her call.

She sank down onto the edge of the bed, and swiped the screen, "Gracie?"

"Yeah, sweetie. I just heard Justin talking to Kaillar, so I figured I'd try to call you now. How are you holding up?"

Becca felt the tears she'd been holding back fall from her eyes, "This is so hard."

"I know. But you're strong enough to get through this. How's your mom handling your dad's death?"

"I guess okay. She ...when I arrived, she met me on the lawn and hugged me. She cried."

"And you?" Gracie asked softly.

"Like a baby. But I don't know that it solves anything. Gracie, there are things that happened...she believes one thing, but..." She couldn't finish talking, the tears were coming so fast that she could barely take a breath.

"Take a breath, Becca. Why don't you tell me what really happened, and then we'll deal with what your mom thinks happened?"

"I don't know that I can. I've never..."

There was a pause and then Gracie softly asked, "Sweetie, have you never talked to anyone about what happened?"

"No. Not really. I mean, I went to see a mental health guy a few times, but that was an utter disaster and I felt even worse afterwards. God, this is so hard."

There was a pause, and then Gracie asked, "Do you believe in God, Becca? I know you used to go to church with Melanie and me from time to time, but I never asked. I didn't want to pry."

"I guess I believe there is a God, but I wasn't raised in church or anything. What about you?"

"Yeah, I believe in God, and I believe that He watches over us and is ready and waiting to help us if we just ask Him for help."

"If that's true, He must not care too much for me."

"Why do you say that?" Gracie asked, wishing she wasn't thousands of miles away.

"You don't know…if God was watching over me four years ago, He must have blinked."

Gracie assured her, "God was watching, but He never promised that we wouldn't go through tough times. Why don't you tell me what really happened four years ago?"

Becca took a small breath, and then began to tell her about Dagan and how she'd fallen head over heels for him. "I really liked him, but it turned out that he wasn't the person I thought he was."

"What happened?"

"He was training on a neighboring island at one of the most dangerous surfing points in the world. My brother and his friend were not quite fifteen, and were the junior champions. They weren't anywhere near ready to take on Pe'ahi size waves, but surfers constantly challenge themselves, and Kevin convinced my parents that he and Kalino would only ride the secondary waves."

"So, you went to this island, and then what happened?"

"Dagan was already there, and he'd told me to find him when we got there because he wanted to talk to me about something. He and his buddies were renting rooms at my parents' resort, but we didn't have a lot of privacy. I was excited, and hopeful that maybe he was going to ask me to go with him when they moved to their summer training grounds."

"That's not what he wanted to talk about?" Gracie asked, trying to keep the conversation moving.

"He didn't actually want to talk. He wanted sex. It sounds horrible, but what he did was horrible. He took me up the beach a ways, and told me we were going to walk, but once we reached the sand, he attacked me. When I fought back, he slapped me, and then tried to choke me as he tried to tear my clothes off."

"Becca? Sweetie, I have to ask, but did he rape you?"

"No. A park ranger heard me cry out and came to investigate. Dagan made up a story about things getting a little out of control, and I was so embarrassed, I didn't say anything. I kept my head down, trying to cope with the fact that my supposed boyfriend had just assaulted me."

"I'm glad his actions were interrupted. Then what happened?"

"He drove us back to the beach, and told me to clean my face up before I joined his friends on the beach. The rental Jeep didn't have any mirrors inside the vehicle, and I didn't think to look in one of the side mirrors. I sat there for a long time, and then went to find my brother and his friend.

"I had decided we were going straight back to the airport and then home. I had every intention of telling my parents some of what had happened, and having them kick Dagan and his buddies off the property."

"Did your parents believe you?"

"I never got the chance to find out. Kevin saw the red mark on my face and the bruising around my throat and took off after Dagan. He'd already started paddling out, and Kevin grabbed his board and gave chase. Kalino heard me yelling at him to stop, and he too headed out after Kevin."

Becca grew silent for a moment, closing her eyes as the events of the next few moments replayed themselves in her mind. "Dagan went out to where the big waves came in, and Kevin followed him. He'd never been in such big water before, but he didn't even pause. This giant wave formed, and Dagan went for it. Kevin tried, but he'd barely gotten to his feet on his board when the wave broke. Right on top of him."

She was crying now, tears streaming down her face. Kalino was too far away to stop him, but also too close to escape the wave's massive power. Dagan wasn't even a match for the wave. He rode it for several seconds before it crashed over him as well. He and Kevin were killed, and Kalino spent three weeks in the hospital in a coma."

"Oh, sweetie! How horrible! Did your parents come…"

"No. Kalino's dad showed up, having heard the call for a medivac over his radio. He found me sitting in the sand, almost catatonic and freezing. He flew me to the hospital where they took Kalino, and my parents were called from there. They drove up to get me, and that's where they learned about Kevin's death.

"My dad was more upset than I'd ever seen him. My mother took one look at me, and immediately assumed the wrong thing. I know she thinks I was off playing games while Kevin was killing himself. The press was horrible. Dagan had been the country's best chance for winning the world title, and now he was dead.

"They had this massive, televised funeral for him. Reporters from around the world showed up. How was I supposed to tell anyone what had happened? Everyone idolized him, and was mourning the loss of one of the best surfers the world had ever known. If I had even breathed a hint of what he'd tried to do, no one would have believed me."

"Your parents…"

"No. They were grieving the loss of their son. My father made sure to let me know that Kevin was his only real child, and that because of me, he no longer had any children."

"But he was your father…"

"Not really. He raised me, but my mom and he never got around to changing my last name. It was and still is Edwards. The way he looked at me was horrible. And my mother, she'd been warning me away from Dagan and his friends. She had firsthand knowledge of the damage the surfer mentality could do to my future. My biological father was a surfer who abandoned her when he found out she was pregnant. In her opinion, I'd ignored her advice, and my brother had paid for my mistake with his life."

A noise from her bedroom door had Becca glancing up to see her mother standing in the partially opened doorway.

Chapter 10

She had a stricken look on her face, and a hand clutching her chest. "Mom?"

Becca dropped the phone when her mother's color drained away, and she collapsed to the floor. "Mom!"

She rushed to her mom, and quickly checked for a pulse. She could hear Gracie yelling at her through the phone, and she quickly crawled back to it before returning to her mom. "Gracie! She collapsed."

"Who?"

"My mom. She was standing in the doorway listening to us talk. She clutched her chest and collapsed. Oh, what do I do?"

"Check for a pulse. Where's Kai?"

Becca glanced down the hallway, and yelled out for him. He stuck his head out of the door a moment later, and rushed to her side. "I can't find a pulse! Oh God, I can't lose her too. Gracie, help me!"

"Whoa! Calm down and check again."

Kaillar took the phone from her hands, and put it on speakerphone, "Hey Gracie! What do I need to do?"

"See if she has a pulse, and get some medical help on the way."

Becca was crying, "Mom! You can't do this. Not now."

"She has a pulse."

"Good. Is it strong and steady?"

"It seems to be. Wait! She's coming around."

"Mom! Can you hear me?" Becca asked, clasping her mom's hand as her eyelids fluttered opened. "Don't move. You passed out. Where do you hurt? Is it your heart?"

Stacie opened her eyes, and then looked at Kaillar before returning her gaze to her daughter. She lifted a hand to Becca's check, "Becca, what you told your friend on the phone…it's just not true. Your father…he never meant for you to take his comments the way you did. It nearly broke him when you left. And I never assumed you were at fault for Kevin's rash actions."

"Dad said…"

"I know what you heard, but he only meant that Kevin was his only biological child. He always loved you as if you were his own flesh and blood. We never had your last name changed because of the difficulty it would have posed with the courts. I would have had to name your biological father, and I wasn't willing to do that. I'm sorry if that choice made you feel less loved."

"I always felt loved. Until Kevin died. It was my fault. If I hadn't gone off with Dagan, he wouldn't have attacked me, and Kevin wouldn't have gone after him."

"Kevin went out there trying to defend your honor?" her mother asked, her eyes clouding with the memory of his loss. "Somehow, that makes his death better. Knowing that he wasn't just being a cocky teenager, taking on too much and trying to grow up too fast."

"No! Kevin would have never attempted those big waves, but he was intent on making Dagan pay for hurting me. I didn't realize that he'd be able to tell anything had happened. It wasn't until I got the hospital and saw my reflection in the bathroom mirror that I saw the bruising he must have seen."

Kaillar picked up Becca's phone and moved back a few feet, taking it off speakerphone. "Gracie, I'll have her call you back later. I think her mother just fainted." Kaillar listened for a moment and then he said, "I'll tell her."

"What?" Becca asked, helping her mom to a sitting position.

"Gracie tells you to remember to only own what's truly yours."

"Good advice. I look forward to meeting this friend of yours one day," her mother commented, using Becca's arm as she got back to her feet.

Stacie looked at her daughter, and then at Kaillar, "We'll talk more about this, but I'm glad to finally know the truth. Now, I think we all need a break from these emotions and memories. Why don't you take one of the Scouts up to the volcano, and show this mainlander the lava flows?"

Becca was amazed that her mother could so easily turn off her emotions. She envied her the ability, but was also grateful to be given a chance to collect herself. She turned to Kai and asked, "Does that sound good?"

Kai nodded, "Yes. Who knows when I'll get another chance to see lava flows."

Stacie gave him a small smile, "Stick around Hawaii too long and you'll see more than lava flows. In the last few weeks, the volcano has been acting up. That usually means an eruption is imminent."

"Why don't you sound more concerned?" he asked, wondering how safe they truly were.

"Kilauea erupts constantly. She can't blow her top, because she already did that. Unless she would really get going, we're in no immediate danger here. Take him up, and show him what I'm talking about."

"Is the crater safe to drive around?" Becca wondered.

"Check at the ranger station. Last report I heard, the crater was still down thirty meters or more."

"We'll do that. Come on. Let's go expand your education about volcanoes and Hawaii." Becca didn't wait to see if he was following her. She darted into the closest bathroom, and grabbed a handful of tissues. She'd already cried off whatever makeup she'd still been wearing when they landed in Honolulu, so she dried her eyes as she headed for the parking area.

A trip up the mountain was just what she needed to remind her that life went on. No matter how bad the circumstances became. It was impossible to view the damage a volcano could cause and not realize that truth.

Chapter 11

Three hours later at the Hawaii Volcanoes National Park Visitor Center...

"This place is amazing," Kaillar told her as they drove along the crater rim. Tendrils of steam and gases rose from the crater in the distance, the landscape looking as if they had been transported to another planet.

The black swirls and folds of cooled lava obliterated the landscape beneath. As far as he could see, the ground was blackened. The remains of trees that had been caught in the fiery flow stood as ghostly reminders that at one point in time, green grass and tall trees had occupied this same location.

"It's a weird feeling, isn't it?" Becca asked, doing her best to put the events of earlier behind her.

"Weird doesn't even come close," Kaillar told her with a look.

"There are some benches up there where we could get out and sit. It might smell a bit if the wind is blowing just right, but if you listen closely, you can hear the sounds from the crater echo across the landscape."

"I'm game." By mutual consent, Kaillar was driving, and he located a vacant parking spot and pulled the vehicle over. As they headed for the benches, it seemed like the most natural thing in the world to reach over and take her hand in his own.

He felt her start, but when she didn't try to reclaim her hand, he silently patted himself on the back. He was making progress, or rather, she was making progress. *Maybe she's beginning to trust me a little.*

They sat in silent contemplation for many minutes. Kaillar was astonished at the young woman sitting next to him. At the age of twenty-three, she'd dealt with more tragedy in her life, and yet she was still trying to move ahead with the act of living. After hearing her story, meeting her mother, and having spoken to Kalino, he realized that while not ideal, her leaving when she did might have been the best thing in some respects.

"So, I know you were feeling very apprehensive about coming home. How are you feeling now?"

Becca gave him a look, and then shook her head, "You sound like Gracie."

"Thank you?" he questioned, trying to keep the mood light.

"It's different than I imagined. I knew that my parents had the wrong idea about what had happened, but things were so tense back then. They were grieving my brother's passing, and it just didn't seem to be getting any better three weeks later.

"When Kalino woke up from his coma, and the doctors said that he would make a full recovery, I realized that I needed to do something different if I ever wanted to be able to say that about my own life. I think my leaving hurt my parents."

"I think that's probably a fair statement. But as you discovered earlier, your mother didn't understand that you had suffered an additional trauma no one knew about. I don't think anyone could have expected you to stay here without some way of dealing with those feelings."

Becca gave him a rueful smile, "But I didn't deal with them. I just locked them away. I thought I was doing a pretty good job of it too, until that attack a few months back. It brought everything back and I realized I'd not gotten rid of any of the guilt."

"Guilt that isn't even yours," he reminded her.

"It's much easier to say that than to believe it's true," she replied with a face.

"I get that. Why don't you let someone else carry the burden for a while?" he suggested, hoping he wasn't stepping over the line with her.

"What? Why would anyone else want to carry around my burden? One you seem convinced isn't even mine to own."

"Because God loves you, and He's the only one that can take the guilt you're feeling and turn it around."

"God again, huh? Gracie went there as well. You really believe in prayer and all that stuff?"

"I do. I've seen it work in my life and in others. Look at it this way; you don't have anything to lose. You did say you believed in God."

"I do, but I don't know that I believe He's the kind of God that takes a personal interest in the lives of his subjects."

"Not subjects. Children." Kaillar thought for a moment, and then explained, "God called us His children. Think of him like a Father. One that only wants good things for His children."

Becca looked at him, and then spoke so softly he could barely hear her, "I've never thought of Him that way. I always envisioned God as this powerful being that watched us like we might watch the nightly news."

Kai smiled at her, "You couldn't be more far from the truth. He wants to be part of your daily life."

"Is He part of yours?" she asked.

"Not in the same way He is with Pastor Jeremy, but – Yes. God is a part of my daily life."

Becca was quiet for a few moments, and then she nodded, "I'll think about it. For now, the wind is shifting, and the smell of rotten eggs doesn't do anything for me."

"I noticed that the odor seems to have gotten stronger. Shall we head back?"

"Yeah. I know my mom said there wasn't anything she needed help with, but I don't believe her. I don't even know what time the service is tomorrow."

"Let's go," Kaillar led her back to the vehicle, and then drove them back down the mountain. He actually felt a sense of relief when green foliage and trees reappeared along the roadway. The devastation done by the volcano was tremendous and yet, as they got closer to the unaffected ground, small plants had begun to push their way up through the charred, hardened lava. The contrast between the black ground and the bright green plants was a great reminder that even though the volcano had destroyed everything in its path, the destruction was only for a time. Life went on, and could flourish even in the midst of such devastation.

He wasn't aware that Becca's thoughts were travelling along that same path. Or that she was doing some serious thinking about this God that both he and Gracie seemed to put so much faith in.

Chapter 12

Sunday, early afternoon…

Kalino and Kaillar stood a short distance away from the closed casket containing the remains of Makoa Kahoalani. The funeral service had been brief, and now all that was left was for Becca and her mother to say their final farewells.

"She's handling this pretty well," Kalino commented to Kai.

"Yesterday was pretty hard on both of them."

"I know. Her mom called me after you both left, and wanted to know why I'd never said anything about Dagan attacking Becca that day. I guess I always assumed that they'd figured it out. By the time I woke up, everything had started to settle down with the media, and Becca was gone. I not only lost my best friend, but Becca had been like an older sister to me. Her leaving felt a lot like I'd been abandoned."

"Didn't you ever think to contact her?" Kai asked, remembering how she'd explained that she'd left her phone number the same and no one had ever called her.

"Her dad told me to leave things alone. That she needed time to deal with everything that had happened, and I assumed he knew her best. I never dreamed that she would stay away for so long."

"Well, I know from talking with her two roommates these last four years that she never even mentioned having a brother. I think she thought if she stayed away, she would never have to deal with the pain."

"That's not how life works. I remember the first time I surfed Pe'ahi after the accident. I stayed away for almost three years. And then one day about a year ago, I realized that if I wanted a shot at winning the Island championship, I'd have to eventually learn how to handle the big waves."

"Isn't that where her brother was killed?" Kai asked.

"Yeah. I watched the forecast, and chose a day where the chances of the waves increasing was minimal. I flew over by myself. I didn't want anyone to see me fail if I chickened out."

"What happened?" Kaillar asked.

"I swam out, and then sat on my board for almost an hour before I got the nerve to make a run for the next wave. I watched surfer after surfer get overtaken in that time. Guys I'd gone to school with, and had competed against for years. Not a one of them was successful in riding the entire wave out."

"Let me guess, that made you more determined than ever to prove that you could do what they couldn't?" Kai asked with a grin.

"Don't you know it," Kalino grinned back at him.

"I'm the same way with downhill racing. Nothing fuels my determination more than watching the skier right before the wipe out."

"There is definitely something wrong with us," Kalino suggested with a broad smile.

"No. We're just competitive. My brother tells me all the time it's going to be my downfall, but I'm also cautious. I assume you are as well?"

"I'm probably the safest surfer I know who still takes on the big ones. If the waves looks too iffy, I'll gladly pass and let someone else take it. The object is to score points. Some of these guys would rather ride for six or seven seconds on a high scoring wave. Not me. I want to go for the thirty second or more ride, on a slightly lower scoring wave. In the end, I score more points, and my parents can sleep at night."

"What are you two up to?" Stacie asked as she and Becca joined them.

"Not much," Kai told her, sobering and watching Becca carefully for signs that she wasn't doing well. Her father had been an island figure, and his funeral had drawn the attention of several reporters from the mainland and Oahu. One of them had recognized Becca, and had been brazen enough to ask her where she'd been hiding. They'd gone on to mention her absence at Dagan's funeral, wondering if she would mind sitting down with them and talking about that tragic time in her life.

Kaillar had instantly become furious, and had stepped between her and the reporters. His sheer size alone had sent them backing up, and the look on his face had warned them not to press their luck. "Miss Edwards will not be giving any interviews. Now or in the future. Please respect her and her family's privacy today."

Becca had given him a grateful look, and then been hustled away by both her mother and Julia.

Kaillar sighed, wishing this ordeal was over for her. "We were just chatting."

Becca nodded, "We're ready to go. Mom's friends should have everything set up back at the house."

"I'm going to ride back with Kalino," Stacie told her daughter. She'd seen the careful way Kaillar kept watch over Becca, and was hoping to give them a few moments alone before they were bombarded by friends of her father's wanting to talk about the man they both respected and loved. It would be a trying afternoon, but also a time to heal and remember the good times.

Kaillar walked her to the car, and then opened the passenger door, squatting down to look into her eyes after she was seated. "How are you really doing, sugar?"

"What is it with you people from Colorado? Gracie calls me sweetie, and you call me sugar. Like I'm a piece of candy or something."

Kai looked hurt, "You don't like it?"

"No, that's not what I meant. I just…sorry, I don't know what I meant."

Kai smirked, "So you do like it when I call you sugar?"

Becca blushed, "Maybe too much. Kai…I don't do relationships…I mean, I haven't in the past four years…"

"Becca, I'm not pushing here. But I think you can tell I really like you. I know you're leery of men in general because of everything that's happened, but I won't ever hurt you like that."

Becca's eyes softened, "I know you won't. I know I kind of scared you the first time we met, but the situation was scary, and when you grabbed me, I didn't know you and it was so much like the parking garage, and…"

"Becca, stop. You don't have to explain anything to me. I am amazed at your strength, and I would understand if you never wanted to trust another man, but I'm hoping that's not the case."

She studied him for a minute, and then she blushed and dropped her eyes.

"What was that thought?" he asked, watching her cheeks turn pink.

"Nothing…"

"Hey! You can tell me to mind my own business, but don't lie to me or to yourself. If you don't want to tell me, I'm okay with that."

She looked up at him, and then bit her bottom lip, looking uncertain before saying, "I was just wondering how you kissed."

73

Kaillar let out a small laugh, and reached out a hand to cup her jaw, "Sugar, how about you stop wondering?" He gave her plenty of time to pull away, but when she only continued to watch him, he dropped his eyes to her mouth and tenderly kissed her soft lips.

He didn't prolong their first kiss, but backed away so he could see her eyes. "How was that?"

"Better than I remembered," she said before she could think about it. When she realized what she'd said, she blushed again and told him, "Sorry. I wasn't meaning to compare you to…"

Kaillar chuckled, "I'm not worried. I know it was good."

Becca laughed in pretend shock, "Conceited much?"

"No. Just honest." He stood up, walked around the vehicle, and got in. Once he had the vehicle running, he turned to her, "Your mom's going to wonder what happened to us."

"Probably, but I also think she designed it this way. She likes you."

"How can you tell?" Kai asked as he pulled out onto the main road.

"I can tell. I may have been gone for four years, but I lived here for nineteen before that. She definitely likes you." *So do I. Maybe too much.*

Chapter 13

Two days later…

"Becca?" Kaillar called out into the backyard. She and her mother had been getting reacquainted for the last two days, and Kalino had been coming around to keep him company. He really liked the young man, and the pair were already making plans for Kalino to travel to Colorado after the holidays to try his hand at skiing.

With his keen sense of balance, Kaillar was sure he'd be a natural. "Becca?"

"Over here," Becca called to him. "What's up?"

"Kalino just called and said there was an outbreak, and you and your mom needed to turn the news on."

Becca nodded her head, and then she and her mom hurried towards the house. They found the local news station, and watched in growing understanding that Kilauea was on the move again and this time, she wasn't going to stop before she did considerable damage.

Reports coming in a few minutes ago show that the outbreak is moving considerably faster than in the past few months. Moving at speeds close to six feet per hour, the lava is going to reach Highway 130 by nightfall. Emergency Response Teams are already in the area, and are urging residents to be on alert for possible evacuation.

"What does all that mean?" Kaillar asked, seeing the worry on the two women's faces.

"It means that if the lava flows comes this direction, all we can do is pack up and leave."

"Six feet per hour seems kind of slow, doesn't it?"

Becca walked over to the refrigerator, and pulled a map of the island off the front. "Kai, this is where the lava flow has currently been held up. It's been building upon itself for the last several months, never making forward progress. This outbreak is off to the side, and moving directly towards Opihikao. Once it crosses the highway, we will only be ten miles or so from its current location."

"Ten miles seems like a lot..."

"Maybe, but the danger that once it starts moving is that it will gain speed as it finds new land to consume. There is also a slight decrease in elevation, which will aid the movement."

"Isn't there anything that can be done?"

Stacie nodded her head, seeming to be unconcerned about the news, "They will install large concrete barriers on the opposite side of the highway to help direct it away from populated areas and residential buildings. It will work in the short term, but if the volcanic activity doesn't slow down, it will only delay the inevitable."

"So, is the resort in danger?"

"At the moment, not really. But in three or four months, maybe. Only God knows the answer to that."

At the mention of God, Kaillar looked at Becca's mom, "You believe in God?"

Stacie smiled, "I was raised in a very nice Catholic orphanage. When I came to Hawaii, I figured God hadn't seen fit to keep me with my birth parents, and I could handle things on my own." She gave Becca a soft smile, "It wasn't until Kevin's death that I realized I hadn't done such a good job. Your father wasn't raised in a church environment like I was, but he still believed in an Eternal Creator.

"After you left, we both had to do some soul searching. Mine led me back to a little non-denominational church in Hilo. I realized that while I'd left God, he'd never left me."

"Mom, I never knew you even thought about God," Becca told her mother.

"I regret that. I do."

Kaillar smiled at Stacie, "Becca and I have been talking about her giving her guilt and feelings of sadness for what happened four years ago over to Him."

Stacie smiled at her daughter, "You won't regret it if you do."

Becca sighed, "I'm still thinking about it."

"Good. Now, I think maybe I need to go have a talk with Julia. We always knew the day might come when the volcano would take back what was hers. We have boxes already in storage, and between the two of us, we've got an evacuation plan all worked out."

"Mom, there's no need to evacuate right now."

"I think maybe there is. Without your father, I don't want to run a resort. A developer gave your father and me a standing offer to purchase the property three months ago. He called me yesterday upon hearing of your father's death, and told me his offer still stands. I'm thinking I will take him up on it."

"But what will you do?" Becca asked, confused at how fast things could change.

"Well, now. I haven't gotten that worked out quite yet, but I will. Now, would you and Kai mind running a few errands for me?"

Kaillar looked at Becca and then answered, "We wouldn't mind at all."

Ten minutes later, he and Becca were headed back into the more populated area of the island surrounding Hilo, "So, she really means to sell?"

"It sounds like it."

"You don't sound very happy."

"I guess I don't like knowing that the resort won't be there the next time I come home."

"Are you planning on coming home more frequently?" Kaillar asked with a smile.

Becca nodded her head, "I think I'd like to see my mom more often. With my dad gone, she only has me now. Julia has plenty of family on the island, but my mom doesn't have anyone."

Kaillar was quiet for a moment and then asked, "Have you considered asking her to come live in Colorado with you?"

Chapter 14

"Colorado? I don't know if she'd even consider it," Becca told him. *Why didn't I think of that? There's nothing really left for her here. If she's going to sell the resort, that might be the perfect time for her to move back to the mainland.*

"Well, maybe you should mention it to her. Justin told me last night that Gracie had been talking to Mason who had been talking to Sarah."

"Sarah with the motel and boarding house?" Becca inquired.

"That's the one. Anyway, the doctor who performed Gracie's knee surgery and Sarah are in love, but Sarah won't even consider moving to Vail until she's found someone to manage the boarding house. Something about leaving the town without adequate accommodations for guests and visiting family members."

"That sounds like Sarah." Becca had stayed with the woman while Gracie was having her surgery, and she'd discovered that the woman had a compulsion to make sure that her guests were completely taken care of. Having been raised around a tourist resort, Becca had seen several things the woman was doing that could be done differently.

"It really does. Anyway, Gracie thought maybe you would be interested in taking over the boarding house for Sarah when you got back. She was going to talk to you the day you got the phone call about your dad."

"Me? But that would mean I'd have to move to Silver Springs…" Becca started laughing, "Gracie thinks she's so smart. She's trying to get me to move up into the mountains!"

"Is that a bad thing?" Kai questioned.

"Not really. I still want to take photos for the Division of Wildlife, but the position isn't full-time, so I'd have to have a second job." *Live in Silver Springs? Where Kaillar lives? Yes, please.*

"Why don't you call Gracie and get the details? Maybe if you had something like that all set up, your mom would feel more comfortable coming to live with you."

"Maybe. She's run that resort for most of my life. A small boarding house like Sarah's would be no problem at all."

Before he could answer, her phone rang and she answered it, "Hello?"

"Hey Becca! It's Kalino. Did you see the news?"

"I did. Thanks for the heads up."

"Yeah. Hey, I'm going to Maui tomorrow, and was wondering if you and Kai wanted to tag along and go sightseeing?"

"Are you surfing?" Becca asked, trepidation in her voice. She wasn't sure if she could watch Kalino surf the same waters that had taken her brother's life or not.

"I am, and while I'd love for you to come watch for a bit, I'll understand if you can't."

Becca looked out the window, and made a snap decision. "We'd love to come, and I'll let you know about the surfing. Kai mentioned to me he wanted to give it a try before we went back to the mainland, but Pe'ahi is no place for beginners."

"Uhm..he didn't tell you?" Kalino asked hesitantly.

"Tell me what?" Becca asked, looking to Kai for answers.

"I'm taking him surfing this afternoon."

Becca smiled and watched Kaillar as she replied, "Really? Now that I will come and see."

"You going to join us?" Kalino asked. "If I remember correctly, you didn't do too badly on a longboard yourself."

"No, I think I'll stay on the beach and take pictures. I'm sure his brothers will pay good money for some good blackmail shots." She could already hear the three brothers bantering back and forth and realized in that moment that she missed that. She also missed her friends and the camaraderie she'd come to love. Moving to Silver Springs wouldn't be any hardship at all.

Kaillar shook his head at her and then whispered, "I'm taking you skiing when we get back to Colorado. Be careful how much retribution you want."

Becca laughed, and agreed to meet Kalino back at the resort after running her mother's errands. It was the first time since arriving on the islands when she actually felt happy and carefree. Whether it was the company, or just the passage of time, she wasn't questioning it. She was just going to enjoy herself.

*****

Later that evening, she watched as Kalino and Kaillar exited the ocean, carrying their boards and with happy grins upon their faces. Kaillar had been a natural, and if she hadn't known better, she would have said he'd been surfing most of his life.

Kalino had been thrilled with how quickly he caught on, and they had taken wave after wave until they were both joyously exhausted.

"That was so awesome! My brothers have got to come over here and try this!"

"Hey, bring them out whenever."

"I will. But before I bring them here, you need to come skiing. Or maybe even snowboarding. Now that would be much easier since you surf. It's a lot like surfing, come to think of it. Both feet on a single board."

Kalino smiled, "Having two different boards to control sounds a little difficult. But snowboarding, yeah – I could get into that."

"Great! Vail Mountain has this awesome half-pipe!"

"If you two are done salivating over your next adrenaline rush, maybe we could go get some food?" Becca told them when there was a break in the conversation.

Kalino and Kaillar shared a look and then they descended upon her, abandoning their towels as they came after her with water still dripping from their heads. When they were close enough, they shook their heads, spreading droplets of water in her direction and causing her to shriek and back up.

She was giggling by the time Kaillar finally caught up with her, Kalino standing off to the side watching her and Kai with a smile upon his face. When she raised an eyebrow at him, he simply stated, "It's nice seeing you smile again, *hoapili*."

Becca's heart melted at the term, and she translated for Kai, "It means close friend."

Kai stepped closer to her and asked, "So is that the term you would use to describe me?"

Becca felt the atmosphere change, and she noticed Kalino stepped away to give them a bit of privacy. She shook her head at him, "No."

Kai lifted a hand to her face, moving a loose tendril of hair behind her ear, "So, how do you say sweetheart in your Hawai'ian?"

Becca fought the urge to close her eyes and tip her head into his caress. "Sweetheart is *ku`uipo*."

Kai repeated the terminology, and then lowered his head, "I want to kiss you again."

Becca gave into the desire to close her eyes and nodded shortly, "Yes."

Chapter 15

Kaillar kissed her softly and then wrapped his arms around her, smiling when she flinched as her body made contact with his cold wet one. When she didn't pull away, but snuggled closer, he thanked God and kissed her again.

He was falling fast and hard for the woman in his arms. He kissed her once more and then let her go, "So, what kind of food do you want to eat?"

Becca was blushing but she met his eyes anyway, "How about traditional Hawai'ian barbeque?"

Kaillar grinned, "Sounds good to me." He turned and waved Kalino over, "Barbeque?"

"You bet. Annie's?" Kalino asked Becca with a grin.

"Is there any other place?" Becca wanted to know. When Kalino shook his head and laughed, she joined in, grabbing Kai and his hands as they headed for the truck. The guys tossed their boards into the bed and then dusted the sand off their feet.

The drive to Annie's only took about ten minutes, and then they were stepping into a small building, the fragrant smells coming from the kitchen had Kai's mouth watering before they were even seated.

The waitress took their drink orders, and then invited them to the food bar. Annie's was an all-you-can-eat food bar with different stations that catered to different types of cuisine. There was a sushi bar, as well as a carving station where the barbeque meat was freshly shaved or cut from the bone.

Kaillar followed Becca and Kalino around the different food stations, taking what looked good, and laughing when Becca occasionally added a spoonful of something to his plate. When she picked up a bowl of what looked like purplish-grey pudding, he made a face and quietly suggested she put it back.

"This is a Hawai'ian tradition and a must try. At least once."

"What is it?" he asked, lifting it to his nose and sniffing it.

"Poi."

"Poi? Dare I ask what it's made from?"

"Taro root. They cook it and then mash it."

Kai looked at the bowl again and then whispered, "What's it taste like?"

Kalino heard his question and stopped, putting his head between the two of them, "Imagine eating warm wall paper paste."

Kaillar looked at him in mock horror. "Really?"

Becca laughed, "Really."

"Why on earth would anyone want to eat wall paper paste?" This time his horror wasn't all for show. There were trays of the stuff, and he couldn't imagine why anyone would willingly eat something so unappetizing when there were all these other choices before them.

Kalino walked by him with a plate laden high with food a moment later, and patted him on the back, "Don't waste too many brain cells trying to figure it out. I've lived here all my life and I still don't understand why anyone without a gun being held to their head would eat that stuff."

"My father's parents ate it with every evening meal. After they passed away, I remember overhearing my mother telling my father she wasn't ever making poi again, and if he had to have it with his evening meal, he could take his evening meals someplace else."

Kalino laughed, "I can see your mom saying that." Becca's mom had a refreshing sense of humor, and Kalino had thoroughly enjoyed hearing her retell exploits from Becca and her brother's youth.

They sat back down, and Kaillar pushed the bowl of poi to the center of the table, "I'm sharing it with everyone. I would hate to deprive either of you of this traditional food."

Becca giggled, "You have to at least taste it once. Just one spoonful. In fact, we'll all take a spoonful together. Deal?"

"I can live with that," Kaillar agreed. The all picked up a spoon and took a small amount on the utensil and then lifted them towards their mouths. "One."

"Two," Kalino said.

"Three," Becca added with a grin. She lifted her spoon up, opened her mouth, and watched as both guys took their bite. Instead of eating her spoonful, she carefully set it aside, watching the faces both guys made as they struggled to get the sticky substance down.

After drinking an entire glass of water, Kaillar looked at her and then shook his head, "No fair."

"Totally fair. Tell me you would willingly take another bite of that stuff."

Kaillar shook his head and whispered, "I wouldn't even let that stuff in my house." He thought for a moment, and then he amended his statement, "Although, I have to admit it would definitely be worth watching Justin and Mason try it."

"We'll get some to take home with us."

Kaillar searched her eyes, "Did you mean Colorado home, or Silver Springs?"

Becca licked her bottom lip and softly answered, "Silver Springs? I spoke with Gracie while you boys were playing in the ocean. She's going to talk to Sarah and work out the details on my behalf. She's also going to contact my landlord and give my notice."

"So now all you need to do is talk to your mom. If nothing else, maybe she would come to Colorado for the holidays."

"Maybe she will." Changing the subject, she asked Kalino, "What time are you wanting to leave tomorrow?"

"Is 8 o'clock too early?"

"Not at all. We'll be at the airport."

"Great." It grew quiet as everyone dug into their food. Light conversation between Kaillar and Kalino about surfing and other mundane things kept the conversation going, giving Becca a chance to just sit back and listen.

She loved how easily Kaillar had fit into her life here. But she wondered if she would find it as easy to fit into his life. She'd seen the girls on the beach staring at him today, and that little devil – jealousy, had risen up inside of her.

She'd hated that they only saw him for a great body, and cared nothing for what lie between his ears. Or about his character. They liked his looks, and that was as deep as they let their relationships get.

That had been Dagan's problem. He'd believed the propaganda that said it was all about looks. He'd believed himself to live by a different set of rules than the rest of the world. Rules that allowed him to act with impunity and without feeling any guilt.

"Are you finished?" Kai asked her a few minutes later.

"Yes. We should probably get back. I'd like to speak with my mom before I go to bed tonight."

"Then that's what we'll do."

"You should keep your eyes open on the drive back. You'll be able to see the glow from the moving lava the darker it gets. That will give us a good idea of how close it really is." Kalino offered the word of caution, knowing that the worry was there in the back of Becca's mind.

Becca nodded her head, "Thanks. We'll do that." She didn't add that she was anxious to get her mom off the island before tragedy could strike the resort. It might not happen this month, and maybe not the next, but at some point in the future, Kilauea would be knocking at the back door of the resort. Becca would prefer that her mother not be there to greet her.

Chapter 16

The next day on Maui…

"So, you two head on up to 'Iao Valley. The Needle is about a two hour hike, but well worth it." Kalino pulled a map of the island from his pack, and tossed it to Becca. "Just in case you've forgotten which trail goes which way."

Becca nodded her head, hoping she wasn't going to embarrass herself by suggesting she and Kaillar go hiking today. She'd given a lot of thought to watching Kalino surf Pe'ahi, and come to the conclusion that she couldn't do it.

He understood completely. He'd suggested she and Kaillar do some hiking, and Kaillar had jumped at the chance to see more of the Hawaiian landscape up close and personal.

"So, there's a small shop just before you enter the park that can rent you packs and anything else you need."

"Great!" Kaillar was a like a kid in a candy store at the mention of packs, climbing ropes, and mountain trails.

Becca nodded again, hoping she hadn't bitten off more than she could chew. She'd been up late last night talking with her mom about the future. Stacie wasn't opposed to moving back to the mainland, and she'd been very interested in the motel and boarding house combination in Silver Springs. But, she was afraid of encroaching on Becca's life. Becca had assured her that she wouldn't have even mentioned it to her if she wasn't onboard with her moving to Colorado.

Stacie had promised to pray about the decision, and let her daughter know before she and Kaillar flew home in two days. Becca had asked Kaillar to schedule their return home, knowing that the longer she stayed, the harder it would be to leave. Her future was in Colorado, not Hawaii, and the sooner she got back on the mainland, the better.

"Ready to go?" Kaillar asked.

"Sure thing." Becca watched the scenery pass by as they headed for the inland road that would take them to the green landscape of the majestic island. She was reminded of those past times when she, Kevin, and Kalino had gone on similar excursions. She loved nature, but she'd allowed the events of four years ago to steal that enjoyment. *No more! I'm taking back my life, starting right now!*

"So, are you really wanting to go hiking?" Becca asked, an alternate plan forming in her mind.

She'd overheard Kaillar talking to Justin and Mason on the phone the night before. He'd had his cell phone on speakerphone and she knew he'd thought he was alone in the house. She'd come inside to grab a light sweater, and when she'd heard her name mentioned, she'd been unable to walk away.

Kaillar had been discussing where he wanted his relationship with her to go. Justin and Mason were both getting married; the final details had all been worked out. Justin and Jessica were getting married in a week and a half in a small ceremony at the Silver Springs church.

Not wanting to steal any thunder from his brother, Mason and Gracie were going to wait until the weekend before Christmas to tie the knot, allowing Justin and Jessica a chance to go on their honeymoon and return.

Both women expected Becca to be in their wedding, and they'd already found and ordered her bridesmaid dress. A single dress for both occasions. Becca had thought the idea brilliant.

The upcoming weddings had evidently started Kaillar thinking about his own future and she'd heard him tell his brothers that he intended to marry her. Their relationship was so new, but because of the circumstances, it had moved very quickly, and Becca knew she'd never find another man like Kaillar. He made her happy, and there wasn't anything about him she didn't like.

The only thing standing in the way was her lack of a relationship with God. Kaillar had been very upset about that. *I can't marry someone who doesn't share my faith. It would be a failure from the start.*

Becca felt badly that she hadn't taken time to tell him about her early mornings with her mother. She'd found her mother a few mornings earlier, sitting on the porch with a cup of hot tea in one hand, and her Bible open in the other.

Her mother hadn't been reading the book, but staring off into space. Becca had joined her, and soon they had begun talking about God, and how her mother had come back to a relationship with Him after her brother's funeral and after Becca had left the Islands.

Becca had always thought her mom a strong individual, and she was shocked to hear her mother admit to being weak and wanting to give up. Stacie shared with her daughter, after the initial shock of Becca leaving had worn off, how self-doubt and self-incrimination had overtaken her thinking. She'd been ready to give up, feeling like a failure.

Becca's dad hadn't fared much better, and it had been Julia who had invited them to the little church she attended faithfully. Becca's mom had recommitted her life to God, and her dad had started his own journey of faith. Together, they had prayed that God would one day bring their daughter back to them and restore their relationship.

Becca had cried, knowing that she'd waited too long to have that with her father. Her mother had held her close, and told her that she knew her father was waiting for her in heaven. She could see him again one day, but the choice was hers.

Becca had pondered those things all day long. That night, as she lay in bed, she'd talked to God for the first time ever. She'd expected to feel silly doing so, but something had happened in her small little bedroom. She hadn't felt silly, and she'd had the strangest feeling that someone was actually listening to her ramblings.

She'd felt comforted, and as she'd drifted off to sleep, she'd felt peace. She couldn't explain it, but she hadn't known whom to ask so she'd called Gracie. Her friend had been thrilled to see her walking down this particular road. She'd made Gracie promise not to say anything, not even to Mason, and Gracie had promised, but refused to let her hang up until she'd prayed for her.

Heavenly Father, you know the hurts Becca has suffered. I ask that right now you would let her feel Your presence in her life. Let her know that You do care and are ready to carry her burdens for her. Let her feel Your love and I ask that You would continue to heal her from the inside out. Show her how much You want to be a part of her life. I ask that You would place people in her path to help show her the way to You.

In Your Holy Name we ask all these things.

Amen

Gracie's prayer continued to roll around in Becca's head, and then she'd heard Justin pray with Kaillar on the phone, using some of the same words with one exception. Justin had prayed that God would give Kaillar the right words, at the right time, to help her find her way. *Instead of praying that God would send someone to help her, Justin was assuming Kaillar was that someone...*

Becca blinked her eyes, suddenly realizing that the vehicle was no longer moving. She glanced around, and then turned to find Kaillar watching her. "Why are we stopped?"

He smirked and then quickly hid it, "So glad you noticed. We've been parked here for almost five minutes."

"What?" Becca glanced around. Here was the side of the road. Here was actually nowhere. "Why did you pull over?"

Kaillar smiled, "Because you were completely zoned out on me. One minute you're asking me if I really want to go hiking, and then you were off on some mental excursion that didn't include me."

"Sorry," she dropped her eyes and sighed. *Way to go there, Becca.*

"So, I'm getting that you'd rather do something other than hike?" Kaillar asked with a smile.

Gathering her courage, she nodded, "Yes. If that's okay with you."

Kaillar smiled at her and nodded, "I don't care what we do. I just want to spend some time alone with you." He leaned across the console and kissed her lightly.

Becca bit her own lip when he drew away. "That's what I want as well. I…" Words failed her as she struggled to tell him what was going on in her brain.

"Hold that thought. Why don't I find us a spot to pull over by the beach, and we can get out and take a walk?" He lifted a hand to her cheek and searched her eyes, picking up on the nervous energy that was swirling around her.

Becca released the breath she'd been holding and nodded. "That sounds really good."

"Great." He started the car moving again, turning off at the first public beach sign they came to. Once parked, he slipped from the vehicle and then assisted her out.

They headed towards the sand, and Becca was relieved to see that this particular beach was almost deserted. Large rocks precluded it from being a safe surfing area, and the beach offered no amenities at all. She slipped her tennis shoes off, and tossed them near a piece of driftwood.

"Aren't you afraid they won't be there when you come back?" Kaillar asked, doing the same with his own shoes.

"There's kind of an unspoken rule about the beaches in Hawaii. We don't mess with other people's things. That includes beach towels, surf boards, and shoes."

Kaillar grinned at her, "Good to know."

Chapter 17

Shoes taken care of, Kaillar grabbed her hand and they started walking, just shy of the water's edge. "So, what's going on in that beautiful mind of yours?"

Becca blushed, "That's a loaded question."

Kaillar grinned down at her, "Give it to me. I can handle it, I promise you."

Becca glanced at him and then took a deep breath, "I heard you last night." She hadn't meant to say it quite like that, but...there it was.

Kaillar didn't say anything for a while and then he asked, "You were eavesdropping on me?"

Becca shook her head, afraid he was upset with her. "No! I came inside to grab a sweater and I heard my name. Then I just couldn't walk away. I heard you and your brother praying for me."

Kaillar looked down at her and asked, "How did that make you feel?"

Becca looked at him and quit walking, "Really? You sound like Dr. Phil."

Kaillar reviewed what he'd said and then chuckled, "Guess I did. But really, were you okay with what you heard?"

Becca nodded and started walking again, "Gracie kind of prayed the same type of thing with me a few mornings ago."

"You called Gracie?" Kaillar asked, curiosity in his voice.

"My mom and I have been talking in the early mornings. About God and stuff. I tried it, and I felt...well, it was strange so I called Gracie. She told me I should talk to either you or my mom, but after last night…" She stopped walking again and looked up at him, "Did you mean what you said?'

Kaillar turned to face her, pulling her close enough that he could put his hands on her shoulders. He moved her hair back off her shoulders, and then nodded, watching her face carefully. "I did. I know that you have lots of concerns, and questions, but I've prayed about it and I think we belong together."

Becca bit her bottom lip and then hazarded a look up at him, "What about the God thing?"

Kaillar pursed his lips for a minute and then sighed, "Yeah. God is a really important part of my life. If He wasn't going to be part of yours as well, we would only have problems down the road."

"I think…," she broke off. Taking a breath, she tried again, "I think I'd like to learn more about Him, but quite frankly, I'm not sure I know how. Gracie would help me, but she's not here."

Kaillar smiled at her, "I'd be more than happy to help you. Let's walk some more." As they walked, Kaillar asked her questions about what she knew and didn't know.

Becca's version of God was as a gamekeeper. He put all the pieces on the board and then just sat back to watch and see what would happen. The God that Kaillar knew was so foreign to her. And yet sounded so perfect. She couldn't imagine anyone having unconditional love. The concept boggled her mind.

"That's where faith comes in. Take for instance surfing. Every surfer has faith when they go out on the water. The same holds true for skiers. We have faith that our equipment is going to work properly. We have faith that the laws of physics aren't going to change. We have faith that we've properly trained and that we have prepared ourselves for the challenge ahead."

"So, believing in God is having faith."

95

Kaillar smiled at her, "Yes! Faith that He's there and cares for us. Faith that no matter what, He will never leave us. Faith that He never gives us a challenge too big to handle."

"But if that's true, that God loves everyone, why does he allow all of these horrible things to happen. And I'm not just talking about Kevin. What about the starving children around the world? Or natural disasters? If He loved us, wouldn't He stop those things from happening?"

Kaillar pulled her into his arms, resting his head on the top of her own, "Those questions have plagued man since the beginning of time. God never promised we'd have an easy life. There are challenges, but overcoming them makes us stronger people. Gives us insight into what others are facing. Helps prepare us for the next challenge we'll face."

Becca listened to his deep baritone voice, loving the image of a loving God he was creating in her mind. When he stopped talking, she pushed away from him and smiled, "I can't promise anything, but I'll try. Gracie said there's a class that meets at the church every week. She thought I might get some answers there."

Kaillar smiled, "You will. Pastor Jeremy and his wife teach the class. It's designed for people who are searching, just like you. Would you like me to call and let him know you'd like to attend?"

Becca nodded her head, "Yes. Uhm…well, uh…would you consider coming with me?"

Kaillar tapped her nose, "Wild horses couldn't keep me away. I'd be honored to come with you. And when you're ready, it will be my honor to pray with you."

Becca snuggled back into his arms and sighed, "Thanks for agreeing to do that with me. And thanks for coming with me here. I know you didn't have to…"

Kaillar nudged her head up again, "That's where you're wrong. I did have to come here with you, like I needed my next breath of air. You stole my heart up on that mountain." He dipped his head and kissed her, drawing the moment out as long as possible.

"So, what shall we do now?" he asked, turning them back to where they'd left their shoes.

"I think maybe I'd like to go watch Kalino surf."

Kaillar looked at her, "You know you don't have to do that. Kalino and I discussed it, and he doesn't want you to do anything that makes things worse."

Becca nodded her head, "I know. But I think I need to do this." She glanced up at him, and then wrapped her arm around his, "Besides, I'll have you there with me."

Kaillar nodded his head after searching her eyes for a long moment, "I will always be there for you, Becca. I want you to know."

Becca laid her head against his shoulder, "I know."

Chapter 18

Two days later, back in Colorado ...

"I'm so tired of sitting," Becca complained as they exited the terminal at the Denver International Airport. They had just flown back from Hawaii and she was more than ready to get home. She took a breath and then shook her head, "It's cold here."

"There's Mason and Gracie," Kaillar told her, waving to his brother and fiancé as they crossed the lanes of traffic.

Gracie was out of the car and hugging Becca before he knew it, and he watched in amusement as the two women hugged and cried on each other's shoulders.

Mason rounded the vehicle and opened the trunk, "Is it always going to be like that with them?"

Kaillar nodded his head, "Yep. I think so. We'd better invest in boxes of tissues."

Mason grinned, and tossed their suitcases into the trunk. "Ladies, I'm glad you all are happy to see one another, but you need to take this little bonding experience into the vehicle."

The two girls broke apart and slipped into the backseat, talking a mile a minute as they tried to catch up on everything. Mason grinned at Kaillar as he pulled away from the terminal, "I now know why those fancy limos have a sliding glass partition in them."

Kaillar looked over his shoulder at Becca, and grinned at the happy look on her face. Her mascara was smeared, and Gracie was handing her a mirror so she could try to repair the damage her tears had done. Again.

"I'm just glad we're home. That's a long flight."

"Well, I hate to be the bearer of bad news, but it's snowing really hard at the tunnel. I don't know that we're getting back to Silver Springs tonight. They've already got the chain law in effect for big trucks, and are advising all non-essential traffic to make other travel plans."

Becca slid forward, "We can stay at my place for one night. Gracie can sleep with me, and you and Mason can take the couch and the second bedroom." She turned back and asked Gracie, "When are the movers coming?"

"Two days from now. They already dropped off some boxes. If we spent the rest of the afternoon, we could probably get most of your stuff packed up."

Becca turned back to the front with a questioning look directed towards Kaillar. "Will that work?"

Kaillar smiled at her, "That will work just fine. Why don't we stop and grab some lunch, and then we can get started?"

Mason nodded and headed towards the foothills. Becca lived in a small suburb on the outskirts of Denver, in a two bedroom apartment. She'd been planning to turn the second bedroom into an office and workroom, but now she wasn't even planning on staying in Denver.

"So, Sarah's okay with everything?" Becca asked.

Gracie nodded, "She's so excited that you and your mom are going to take over her place. When is your mom coming?"

Becca smiled at her, "Well, she closes on the resort Friday. Julia, my mom's longtime friend is going to come with her. I want to be able to focus on my photography and this way, mom won't have to manage the guests by herself."

"That's a great idea. Sarah already has her stuff packed for her move to Vail. She and Stan are flying to Las Vegas next week to get married."

"That's quick," Becca commented, causing both Mason and Kaillar to laugh. "Why is that so funny?"

"Stan and Sarah have been dating, long distance, for almost seven months. With his schedule at the hospital in Vail, and her commitment to the motel and boarding house, they've only been able to see each other a few times each month."

"That's hard. How do you keep a relationship going long distance like that?" Becca asked.

"You have to truly love the other person. But I agree," Gracie told her, "That would be the hard way to have a relationship."

Becca thought for a moment, and then she brightened, "What if we put together a small celebration for when they return from Vegas? We could use the common room at the motel and invite some of Dr. Geske's friends from Vail."

"Becca, that's a great idea," Mason told her, directing the vehicle into the drive-thru of a popular burger joint.

"I'm sure both Stan and Sarah would appreciate that," Kaillar told her with a proud smile on his face.

Mason pulled up to the order spot and then asked, "What does everyone want?"

After receiving their food, Mason drove them straight to Becca's apartment. They ate amidst talk about Hawai'i, and Kaillar spent most of his time talking about surfing. "Becca's friend is really good and I think I've convinced him to fly out here after the holidays and try his hand at snowboarding."

"Kalino is looking forward to it," Becca told him. "He texted me to find out what kind of arrangements he needs to make for lodging. I told him I'd talk with you and not to worry about it."

Kaillar nodded, "Yeah. He can room at the lodge, or even down at the motel. Next time you talk to him, remind him that we'll need his flight schedule so that someone can meet him at the airport."

"Why don't I just give you his cell phone number and you and he can work out the details?" Becca asked.

Kaillar chuckled and handed her his phone. "That sounds fine."

They split up after that, the girls taking the kitchen, and the boys heading towards the hall closet and living room. Their focus was to deconstruct the electronics and pack them correctly into the moving boxes.

Gracie and Becca made short work of the kitchen cabinets, and then they headed for the bathroom and linen closet. As they were working, Gracie asked questions about Becca's time on the Island, and Becca found herself completely opening up. About everything.

"Kaillar was really supportive through everything."

"Meaning what?" Gracie asked.

Becca put the towels she was holding in her hands into a box, and then she told Gracie about their walk along the beach. "He spoke to Pastor Jeremy. There's a class meeting Sunday afternoon he thought might be a good fit for me."

"Are you nervous?" Gracie asked, remembering how nervous and unsure of herself Gracie had been.

"A bit, but not about meeting new people. I just don't want to let Kaillar down. Or myself."

Gracie stopped what she was doing and asked, "How do you think you're going to let anyone down?"

Becca shrugged, "I don't really know. But if this doesn't work.."

"This? You mean a relationship with God? That's what you think might not work?"

Becca nodded, "Why are you looking at me like that?"

Gracie burst out laughing, "Oh Becca. You don't have to worry about it not working out when it comes to God. He wants to have a relationship with you so badly. Did you and Kaillar talk about how it all works?"

Becca shook her head, and Gracie repeated the gesture. "Men. Leave them to do one thing right. Come with me and let's take a small break." She pulled her back out to the living room, and sat them both down on the couch.

Gracie began to tell her about the price that had already been paid for her. At one point, Mason and Kaillar started to come into the living room, but after seeing the two women sitting on the couch, their heads bent close together, and an open Bible sitting on Gracie's equipment, they had retreated to the bedrooms to begin packing up the contents of the closets.

"She's going to be fine," Mason told his brother. "You know that, right?"

Kaillar nodded his head, "I hope so. I really do."

Chapter 19

One week later, back in Silver Springs…

Pastor Jeremy walked Becca out of the church, "Becca, I can't tell you how happy I am that you've chosen to stay in Silver Springs with us. I'm really looking forward to meeting your mother and her friend as well."

"Thanks Pastor. And thanks for that in there. I was so nervous, and now I don't even remember why." Becca had a broad smile upon her face, and she couldn't wait to see Kaillar. She looked around and then frowned, "I wonder where my ride is?"

Before Pastor Jeremy could answer her, a truck pulled up and Justin climbed out, "Becca, are you ready to go?"

She nodded, "Where's Kaillar?"

"He and Mason are on their way down the mountain. Pastor, tomorrow's the big day."

"Yes. Are you and your bride ready to get married?"

"Jessica is stressed out. She keeps telling me there is so much to do, but really, all she needs to do is show up. Nothing else matters."

Becca shook her head at him, "That's why guys are never put in charge of things like this. Left up to you, she'd probably be getting married in a pair of sweats and a T-shirt."

Justin shook his head, "No. I amend my statement. I'm dying to see this dress she found."

Becca sighed, "Me too. Gracie's dress is pretty cool as well."

Justin grinned, "So when are you going to be heading into Denver to find the perfect dress?"

Becca blushed, "I don't know. Your brother and I are taking things slow."

"What's to take slow? You love each other, get on with your lives."

Pastor Jeremy laughed at that, "Justin, you're not helping our cause at all. I'm sure Kaillar and Becca will move their relationship forward when the time is right."

*****

That time came the next afternoon. Justin and Jessica's wedding had been amazing. This close to the holidays, Jessica had gone with pine boughs, holly berries, and poinsettias instead of flowers. All except for her bridal bouquet.

That had been a mixture of pine fronds, little sprigs of red berries, and white calla lilies brought in from a greenhouse in Denver. They had draped beautifully from her hands, and Becca thought she was the most beautiful bride ever.

Her mother and Julia had called an hour earlier to say that they had landed safely in Denver. Her mother had sold everything before leaving Hawaii, and was now going to take a few days to find a new vehicle.

Her father had maintained a substantial life insurance policy, and with the sale of the resort, her mother could well afford to buy herself a new car. The Donnelly Brothers had insisted that she purchase an SUV with four wheel drive. The chances that her mother would ever use that feature seemed unlikely, but then again…this was Colorado, and they did live in the mountains.

Kaillar came up behind her and wrapped an arm around her waist, nuzzling her ear, "You look beautiful this afternoon."

Becca glanced up at him and smiled, "Thank you kind sir. This dress is amazing."

Kaillar spun her around and perused her from the top of her strawberry blonde hair that had been expertly braided and wound around her head to the tips of her ivory boots. Becca was wearing the bridal dress the girls had picked out for her, and they couldn't have done a better job. It was a deep emerald green, almost matching her own pale eyes, and causing them to shine brightly. A soft velvet fabric that clung to her curves, and yet was loose enough to be comfortable.

They'd chosen a long gown, with a high low hemline, letting her ivory boots peek out from the front, and the material of the skirt slightly dragging behind when she stood still. "Beautiful," Kaillar told her once more before taking her hand and leading her out the back door of the church.

"Where are we going?"

"I want to show you something." He pulled her behind him, snagging two jackets off the rack on his way.

"Kaillar! Those aren't ours."

"Doesn't matter. It's too cold to stay outside for long, and we'll put them back. Slip this on." He handed her the smaller of the two jackets, and she dutifully slipped her arms into it.

He took her hand again, and pushed through the glass doors. It was dark outside, the back of the church having outdoors lights, but they had not been turned on. He continued pulling her along the shoveled sidewalk, almost two feet of snow rising on either side.

Becca shivered a bit, but the stillness of the night begged her not to utter a word of protest. She followed along, feeling a sense of excitement in the air, but not knowing why.

Kaillar finally stopped in the middle of a small courtyard and turned to face her. "Look up," he encouraged her.

Becca slowly tipped her head back and then gasped in awe. The sky was alight with stars! She let her eyes track the night sky, the absence of artificial light and clouds letting the entire Milky Way appear for her to appreciate.

"Wow!" she whispered reverently. "That's the most beautiful thing…"

"No. You are the most beautiful thing. Becca?"

She took one more look, and then tipped her head down to see Kaillar down on one knee with a small velvet box held out to her. She covered her mouth with her hands, searching his eyes for answers.

Kaillar watched her eyes fill with what he hoped were happy tears, and hurried to get his words out before she started crying. That was something he was slowly getting used to, but barely. He hated seeing her cry, and it didn't matter if they were happy tears or not.

"Becca Edwards, those stars above don't hold a candle to how you light up my life. I know we need time to grow as a couple, but I can't go another minute without knowing that you're going to be mine. One day."

"Would you do me the extraordinary honor of agreeing to be my bride? To live here in this mountain town with me? To support me as I support you? To raise a family with me here?"

The tears won out and spilled from her eyes even as she nodded her head and whispered, "Yes. I love you too."

Kaillar surged to his feet and swept her up in his arms, kissing her to celebrate their newfound commitment. "Thank you. My number one goal in life is going to make you so happy, you run out of tears." He removed the ring from the box, and slipped it on her finger.

Becca smiled at him and then kissed him again, "Kai, you are the most amazing man I've ever met. I thank God every day for bringing you into my life."

Kaillar hugged her close, "As do I." He closed his eyes and then softly started to pray. For the healing that Becca was experiencing. For restoring her relationship with her mother, and for coming home to God. For bringing the perfect woman into his life, and providing him with just the right answers at the right time.

Becca started shivering, and he hustled them both back inside, returning the borrowed jackets, and then taking her hand and leading her back inside the reception. She was glowing with happiness, and he wasn't surprised at all when both Gracie and Jessica crossed the room and wrapped her in a hug.

He took the box of tissues Mason produced, and handed them to the women. The tears were already flowing. "I'm telling you, we need to invest in a company that makes tissues. Can you imagine what they're going to be like when kids start arriving?"

Mason grinned, "Beautiful. And crying."

Kaillar chuckled, and then retrieved his new fiancé from the small circle of women, "Sorry girls, but she's mine. Jessica, go cry on your husband. Mason, you and Gracie will be getting married in another week and a half."

Mason smiled, watching as Justin joined them. "Lose something, brother?"

Justin smiled and pulled Jessica into his arms, "No. I knew she was just over here getting rid of any extra tears she might have stored up. You girls need to figure out another way to express your emotions. Every time we see tears falling from your beautiful eyes, it breaks our heart."

"These were happy tears," Becca told him softly, liking the feel of having Kaillar's arms wrapped around her waist.

He bent his head to whisper next to her ear, "Doesn't matter, sugar. It still breaks our hearts."

Becca glanced up at him and promised, "I'll try not to cry as much."

He smiled, "Go ahead and cry. Then I have an excuse to offer you the comfort of my arms."

Becca grinned and realized his brothers were taking advantage of the situation as well. She looked at the other two couples, and couldn't believe how much her life had changed in such a short amount of time. Three weeks earlier, she'd been looking at living alone in Denver, no firm job prospect in mind, and both of her friends moving to other cities.

Now she was getting married, going to be running a motel and boarding house with her mother and family friend Julia, and living in a town that was so special to her. Silver Springs might be a small town, but the miracles that had been wrought in her life because of this small town were anything but small.

Epilogue

Five months later, Saturday morning in early May at the Three Brother's Lodge...

"I'm sad the school year is almost over," Jessica said to the room in general as she helped bring food to the table. She and Justin had been married in the first part of December, with Gracie and Mason following a week and a half later.

Mason had moved to town with Gracie, taking over the second master suite in the William's house. As the town doctor, she felt that it was important for her to be close to her office, and Mason had readily agreed. The school board had leased the property for their new school teacher, Jessica, and there were still times when she and Justin stayed in town, especially on nights when the weather turned foul, and driving up and down the mountain to get her to school was dangerous.

Kaillar and Becca had gotten married the second Saturday in March. It had been a cold and blustery day outside, with snow falling, and grey clouds blotting out the sunshine. But inside the small church, flowers had been blooming, and love had flowed around them as they celebrated the beginning of their married life.

That had been two months ago, and as had become custom, all three couples were at the lodge for the weekend. While the girls made brunch, the guys had gone out to take care of the chores. Everyone was working well together, and these times were always the highlight of not just Becca's week, but everyone seemed to look forward to them.

"That just about does it," Becca told the other two women. Before anyone could reply, the front doors opened, and the three men came walking in.

"Breakfast smells amazing," Kaillar told her as he joined her and kissed her on the cheek.

Justin kissed Jessica and took a seat at the table, pulling her down to sit beside him. Mason and Gracie took seats on the opposite side of the table, and soon everyone was enjoying good food and good company.

"I was thinking that we could saddle up the horses and go for a ride after we eat," Justin suggested.

Mason and Kaillar both nodded their heads before Mason turned to Gracie, Sounds good, huh?"

"Sounds fun, but I think I'll stick around here this morning. I've got just a few work things I need to clear up so I can enjoy the rest of the weekend."

Mason looked disappointed, "Are you sure?"

Gracie smiled at him and nodded, "I'm sure."

Justin took Jessica's hand, "You up for a ride?"

Jessica shook her head, "I think I might stay here as well. You guys go and take Becca with you. I'll even start lunch while you're all out."

"Mac and cheese?" he asked with a grin.

"Sure. Mac and cheese it is."

"Uhm…I think I'll stick around as well. But you guys go and have fun," Becca said in a too bright voice.

"Becca, you like to ride. Now anyways. Come with us…"

Becca shook her head, "I really shouldn't….I mean, I can't…" She was stammering all over herself trying to come up with a reason to not go riding. She didn't do a good enough job, and Kaillar narrowed his eyes at her.

"What's going on?"

"Yeah, I think I might like to ask the same question," Mason replied, watching his wife carefully.

Becca blushed and then shook her head, "Nothing is going on."

"You're hiding something."

Her blush intensified, and she closed her eyes and wished she'd practiced being a better liar. "I just don't want to go riding. Not today."

Kaillar watched her, suspicion lurking in his eyes before he asked, "And when might you feel like going riding."

Becca smiled up at him, realizing he was putting two and two together, and coming up with five. "Maybe another six months, give or take a few weeks."

"You're pregnant?" Gracie asked, joy lighting up her features.

Becca nodded, "I think so."

Gracie beamed at her, and then whispered to the room in general, her eyes firmly fixed on her husband, "We can raise our children together then. I'm two months pregnant as well."

Mason looked at Kaillar, who was still watching his wife with a mixture of shock and approval. "Well, here I thought we might be to a point where I didn't have to pack a box of tissues around with me. Guess I was wrong."

Kaillar shook his head, and looked at Jessica. "Don't tell me you're pregnant as well?"

Jessica stuck her tongue out at him and tossed her hair, "Fine I won't. Justin dear, I'm pregnant."

Becca, Gracie, and Jessica were all crying by this time and chattering away about how close their children were going to be. "This is so cool!"

The three men finished their brunch, and then headed out for a ride. When they were standing on the top of the ridge, overlooking the mountains and valleys below and in the distance, Justin finally spoke up.

"What are the odds that we would all find the loves of our lives within a few weeks of one another? And now, we're all going to have children."

Mason grinned, "What do you think Uncle Jed would say if he could be here right now?"

The three men were quiet for several long moments. Finally, Justin spoke up. "I think he'd remind us of all the life lessons we learned. How to be a good steward of the land and resources. How to love the Lord and our family."

"But most of all, I think he'd remind us that children need to be nurtured and led in the right direction. He'd remind us to always be good role models. And I think he'd tell us how proud he is of the men we've become."

Justin looked at his brothers, one on either side of him and laughed, "The Donnelly Brothers are going to be daddies!"

Mason whooped and laughed. Kaillar tipped his head back and howled. "God has been very good to us."

Justin and Mason agreed. "He sure has been. Now, I say we go back to the lodge and spend some time with our women. Hopefully by now they've stopped crying."

"Don't bank on it. They're probably already planning nurseries and playdates."

Mason frowned, "You think so? That means they'll expect us to put together cribs and changing tables, and whatever else they can find."

"Welcome to fatherhood, boys!" Justin told them, turning his horse around and heading back to the lodge. He'd take whatever blessings God sent him and Jessica's way.

Once they had taken care of their horses, he stopped and waited for Mason and Kaillar to join him. "Boys, we're going to be much better parents to our kids than our mom even tried to be. Uncle Jed was only one man, and he taught us well. Our children are going to be the most loved kids in the county."

Becca, Gracie and Jessica were standing on the front porch and overheard his comment. "We already feel like the most loved women in the county," Gracie called out.

"Good." Each man collected his wife, and soon they were sitting around the living room, making plans for workdays and deciding where they were going to put a nursery. When Stacie and Julia walked in several hours later, the boys accepted their congratulations, and then each man handed their wife their own box of tissues.

Life was good, and they were living proof that God could take any situation and turn it around for good. The Three Brothers Lodge was intact and would be for generations to come. Filled with love and the promise of God's blessing over their lives.

Thank You

Dear Reader,

Thank you for choosing to read my books out of the thousands that merit reading. I recognize that reading takes time and quietness, so I am grateful that you have designed your lives to allow for this enriching endeavor, whatever the book's title and subject.

Now more than ever before, Amazon reviews and Social Media play vital role in helping individuals make their reading choices. If any of my books have moved you, inspired you, or educated you, please share your reactions with others by posting an Amazon review as well as via email, Facebook, Twitter, Goodreads, -- or even old-fashioned face-to-face conversation! And when you receive my announcement of my new book, please pass it along. Thank you.

For updates about New Releases, as well as exclusive promotions, visit my website and sign up for the VIP mailing list. Click here to get started: www.morrisfenrisbooks.com

I invite you to connect with me through Social media:

1. Facebook :
   https://www.facebook.com/AuthorMorrisFenris/
2. Twitter: https://twitter.com/morris_fenris
3. Pinterest: https://www.pinterest.com/AuthorMorris/
4. Instagram:
   https://www.instagram.com/authormorrisfenris/

For my portfolio of books on Amazon, please visit my Author Page:

Amazon USA:
amazon.com/author/morrisfenris

Amazon UK:
https://www.amazon.co.uk/MorrisFenris/e/B00FXLWKRC

You can also contact me by email:
authormorrisfenris@gmail.com

With profound gratitude, and with hope for your continued reading pleasure,

Morris Fenris
Author & Publisher

Printed in Great Britain
by Amazon